A wide-eyed punk sprinted up the stairs, Kalashnikov flashing.

Lyons fired two rounds point-blank into the punk's chest.

Flesh exploded from the teenager's back as he slammed sideways into the stairwell. But he did not fall down.

Instead he saw Lyons and Blancanales and raised his AK as blood sprayed from lung wounds.

Lyons put the muzzle of his rifle under the punk's chin and fired. The blast tore away the side of the punk's head, but still he did not fall.

He lurched forward, aiming his gun, obviously not feeling the horrible wounds. At last a burst from Gadgets's Uzi severed the brain from the spinal cord.

Gadgets stared at the dead youth, then pointed down the stairs to where more drug-mad punks lay in wait.

"I don't care what you say, Lyons. You can call an airstrike, call for tanks, call for Marines, but *I'm not going down there!*"

Mack Bolan's
ABLE TEAM

Mack Bolan's
PHOENIX FORCE

MACK BOLAN
The Executioner

ABLE TEAM

AN EXECUTIONER SERIES

Army of Devils

Dick Stivers

A GOLD EAGLE BOOK FROM
WORLDWIDE

TORONTO · NEW YORK · LONDON · PARIS
AMSTERDAM · STOCKHOLM · HAMBURG
ATHENS · MILAN · TOKYO · SYDNEY

First edition October 1983

ISBN 0-373-61208-7

Special thanks and acknowledgment to G.H. Frost
for his contributions to this work.

Printed in Canada

1

A machete slash severed her hand. Blood pulsed from the stump to splash the sorority-house door and security chain.

Peggy Miller, an eighteen-year-old freshman student of cinema at the University of Southern California, daughter of a New York advertising executive, stared with disbelief at the wound. As a lifelong television and movie addict, she had seen uncounted thousands of murders and mutilations. As a devotee of the horror genre, she had already made films of the macabre and terrifying, sometimes appearing in front of the camera, other times writing the script or operating the camera or serving as a makeup artist to create the images of suffering and mutilation and grotesque death.

Often she had giggled at the sight of movie blood splashing. She had twisted her face into a mask of manic rage and hacked at the other actors and actresses with plastic knives and axes. After the scene, they all laughed, the syrupy blood sticky on their bodies. Once, she had endured ten retakes of her own murder as the student director struggled to capture the *vérité* of vivisection by electric carving knife on Super-8. That evening, Peggy and a handsome young actor ended the shooting day with a private orgy in a Jacuzzi, licking away the sweet phony blood caking their hair and bodies, their lovemaking leaving a puddle of sweat and cinema blood on the tiles.

But now, a real wound spurted blood. As the image and the first horrifying sensations of pain registered in her numbed mind, she saw her hand on the floor. Fingers curling upward, the hand lay on the Persian entry carpet, its dead flesh a startling white against the colored designs of the hand-woven carpet.

The machete blade hacked again and again at the security chain. But the chain held. A voice that came from a throat that could not be human made a low, bestial grunt, then the door splintered. One attacker after another crashed through the broken door.

In the last seconds of her life, Peggy Miller faced a gang of punks beyond the imagination of any casting director. They wore the uniform of the streets: boots, black jeans, black nylon jackets, bandannas tied over their faces and hair. Their eyes stared out from the gap between the bandannas.

Psychopathic hatred raged in those eyes.

Even as her reflexes raised her arms to push away the monsters rushing her, as a scream rose in her throat, Peggy Miller surrendered to death.

tes reduced her to a headless, armless corpse kicking with nerve spasms. As two punks continued hacking at the body, more of them rushed into the other rooms of the sorority house.

One punk ran into the white tiled kitchen. A young woman in a purple silk kimono turned from the refrigerator. Before her scream came, a machete blade axed through her brain.

A blaring stereo led two punks to a first-floor bedroom. Snapping the lightweight bolt with a kick, the punks saw two forms in two beds. The awakened sleepers jerked upright.

"Get out! What—"

"Who—"

Machetes ended the protests of the young women. Not content with murder, the gang boys continued chopping at the naked girls. Laughing as they hacked, they reduced the bodies to an intermingled mass of meat and entrails.

A scream pierced the rock and roll. In the living room, a young woman in a red velour sweat suit ran for the stairs. A shotgun blast tore her legs, throwing her down hard on the carpeted steps. Clawing at the carpet, she screamed when she attempted to crawl on her shattered legs. She suffered only a moment longer.

Rushing up to the bleeding young student, the masked punk pumped the sawed-off shotgun's action. She screamed at the grinning monster. He put the muzzle of the 12-gauge shotgun to her face.

Brains and bone fragments sprayed the stairs. Laughing at the gore, the gang punk sat down on the blood-soaked carpeting of the step. He kicked the headless body away. Taking a hand-rolled cigarette from his jacket pocket, he pulled down the red bandanna from his face.

It bore the scars of innumerable street fights. The young black man's front teeth had been knocked out by fists. Scar tissue hooded one eye, giving him a permanent squint. His breath whistled through a smashed nose. A knife slash had scarred his cheek and ear, the straight line disappearing into the matted hair under the bandanna that covered the top of his head.

Lighting the cigarette with a silver lighter—stolen from a tourist in downtown Los Angeles—he sucked down a long drag of the drug. His eyes closed, his face went slack. The cigarette clung to his lip as he fell back against the steps. He exhaled and pulled down another drag.

For seconds he lay motionless. The glowing point of the cigarette burned into his chin, but he did not move. Finally, his breath escaped in a slow swirl of smoke.

One hand caressed the shotgun. His eyes opened. A piece of skin came away from his chin as he took the cigarette from his lip. He carefully stubbed out the half-gone cigarette.

Screams and sobbing came from above him. He turned to the sound, his lips pulled back in a rictus grin of broken and decayed teeth. The tendons and blood vessels in his throat stood from the flesh as a visible wave of loathing and psychopathic murder-lust moved through him. Somewhere on the second floor, a machete stopped the crying.

Laughing again, he pulled up the bandanna to cover his face. Through the thin cotton cloth, he could hear the laughter continue. As he pumped another shell into the chamber of his sawed-off 12-gauge and went up the stairs, he hissed, "Die, honky sluts...."

RAOUL VALENCIA, a red-haired young Mexican from the state of Michoacan, turned the ignition key for the tenth time. But nothing. No response from the starter motor, no lights, no emergency blinker.

Only an arm's distance to his left, the headlights of Harbor Freeway traffic flashed past at sixty miles an hour. His boys—Miguel and Thomas—sat in the back seat, staring back at the onrushing traffic. His wife, Maria, held their youngest in her arms, as if to protect the baby girl from the rushing tons of metal threatening the Valencias with disaster.

When the old Buick's electrical system had failed, Raoul fought to guide the car out of traffic. Though he would not admit it even to Maria, that long moment, from the speed lane to the side of the freeway—without power, without lights, without brakes, the other cars skidding and swerving around him, his family so close to death—had been the most terrifying thirty seconds of his life. His mouth had gone dry with fear.

The sprint across the border at Juarez had been nothing. So what if the American *federales* took him? It had been a quick bus trip across the border and another swim and run the next night. Nor had he felt fear during the long, anxious wait for the *coyote* to smuggle Maria and the boys across. His brother had trusted the *coyote* with his money and his life; his brother had crossed without a problem. No, Juan-the-coyote did not abandon people to die in the desert. Nor did he molest the wives of other men. A man of honor. He earned his money honestly. Raoul had not feared.

But when the car quit! Ayiii!

By the grace of the Virgin, they had reached the safety of the roadside. Now to start the Buick. . . .

He must do it before the highway police stopped to help him. What if they asked for his papers?

To lose it all now—capture in Los Angeles meant return to Mexico City.

No matter. Even if the American authorities sent him back, he would return.

Taking a flashlight from under the seat, Raoul waited until no headlights threatened him, then quickly left the car. He dashed to the front of the Buick. Untying the rope that replaced the latch, he threw the hood open.

The battery cable had broken.

No problem. Use a jumper cable to replace the

battery cable. He wished bleakly that his neighbor from Haiti had accompanied him on this journey, because of the arrangement to use a car. Raoul had fixed Jean-Claude's wreck of a Chevy back home many times.

Haiti—now there was a problem. To be returned to Mexico was not good. A visit with relatives, then perhaps a week or month of travel before crossing the border again. But Haiti? Jean-Claude had told Raoul of the boats drifting in the ocean, of the many dying, of the fear of return to the torture chambers.

Raoul thanked God for his Mexican birth as he went to the trunk. He took out one of the jumper cables.

Headlights illuminated the rear of the Buick. Jumping aside, Raoul looked back to see a car slowing to a stop.

Highway police? A tow truck? He could not see through the glare of the high beams. He waited with his hands in sight—he did not want any pistol misunderstandings with the police.

Raoul Valencia never heard the shots that killed him. Thrown backward ten feet by the impact of a double-barreled blast, he died before his wife screamed.

Gang punks swarmed from the idling car. The driver waited, revving the engine, his hand on the gearshift, as the others smashed the windows of the Buick. One punk grabbed Maria Valencia by the hair and tried to drag her out. Her eight-year-old firstborn son, Miguel, beat at the attacker with his tiny fists.

A punk shoved a short-bladed sword through the boy's body. Another punk fired a .38-caliber revolver wildly into the back seat, hitting six-year-old Thomas.

Maria fought to protect her baby. The punks laughed at her screams, finally dragged her out. They tore the baby from her arms.

As hundreds of cars passed only steps away, the gang raped the young mother in the roadside darkness, then hacked her to death.

The gang escaped in their metal-flaked and lowered Chevrolet. Careering south on the Harbor Freeway at eighty miles an hour, they smoked cigarettes of an acrid-stinking synthetic drug.

When they tired of tossing Maria's baby among themselves like a ball, they threw it out the window.

Lou Stevens listened to his grandson cry. He heard the oak floor creak as his daughter paced the bedroom with the baby in her arms, crooning to quiet his cries.

In the years since his wife died, Stevens had lived alone. Though the neighborhood people knew him as a man unchanging in his daily routine, he welcomed the disruption of his daughter and son-in-law's visit to show him his grandson. . . .

His chairmanship of his corporation did not allow Stevens the time to visit his daughter and son-in-law in the East. Therefore, he had persuaded them to take the money for the air fares and lost wages. Their visit came at an inconvenient time now, but he would not postpone their trip. If the company objected to his limited concentration on the pressing business of microprocessors, let the board vote him into retirement.

In the late night silence, lying alone in the darkness of his bedroom, Stevens listened to his blood pulse in his ears. He felt the rhythm of his heart. Sixty-one years old, he did not imagine himself immortal. After fifty years of work, forty years in electronics, twenty years as a manager in a high-stress industry, he knew he neared the end. He had seen men ten years younger than he was drop on the office floor and die before the paramedics arrived.

But in one lifetime, he had climbed from the gutter to within grabbing distance of the upper class. Self-educated—with the assistance of the U.S. Army Signal Corps and the G.I. Bill—he had learned to design circuits. When companies refused to share the profits of his imagination, he formed his own company dedicated to the opportunity to achieve and to receive a fair reward. His patents and the patents of the young engineers staffing his research and development labs now earned more profits than his company's manufacturing division.

Though his daughter and poet son refused his offers of guaranteed positions with his company—

he had listened to their refusals with pride—Stevens would not give them the opportunity to refuse their inheritance. He had no fear they would squander the money. In their own ways, they reflected his puritan discipline and creative drive. His son won award after prestigious award for his poetry, while sacrificing the tenure and financial security of a university to devote his genius to full-time writing. His daughter had invested ten years of Spartan existence to win post-graduate honors at her university, then pre-eminence at a foundation dedicated to the study of emerging modern culture.

Neither of his kids made any money. None of his friends ever opened the books of his son's poetry that Stevens gave away by the hundreds. And he could not even tell his friends what his daughter studied—he never understood her explanations.

Alone in the dark, listening to the crying of his grandson and the singing of his daughter, Stevens realized he had not been so happy in years. He regretted only that his wife had not lived to see their victory.

Lou Stevens thought of his life and wealth as a victory over impossible odds. As if in a vivid and brilliantly colored dream, he remembered going through the trash of Los Angeles neighborhoods to find discarded electrical appliances. He hit the cans first with a stick to chase out the rats, then searched for appliances and wire and bits of metal he could sell as scrap. Many years ago....

Music blasted the street's quiet. Music, ha! Stevens snorted in the dark. How can kids think that electronic shrieking is music?

Stevens laughed at himself. Your designs and components, mister. That kind of music will pay for the boy's schooling twenty years from now.

A car door slammed. Other doors slammed. Raucous laughter became hyena cackles. The sound of those voices made Stevens's body flash cold. He sat up in bed. He often lay awake all night worrying over business and technological problems. He knew the voices of every neighbor on the block.

He did not recognize the voices in the street. Going to the window, he eased the drapery aside an inch.

Four figures in black walked to his home's gate. One pointed to the new Cadillac in the driveway. They laughed. In the street, the passenger-side front door of their lowered car opened.

In the moment that the dome light revealed the interior, he saw two young men in the front seat. One wore bandannas over his hair and face, leaving only his eyes exposed. The driver, a young black man with a mass of ratted hair, waited behind the steering wheel.

The bandanna-masked teenager carried a sawed-off shotgun.

Heart pounding in his chest, Stevens saw the four shadows at the front of his house vault the low fence. They walked through the flowers to his front door.

In his pajamas, Stevens went to his bedroom door. He stopped. He went back to his bed and reached underneath. By touch, he disconnected the electronic alarm and tear-gas booby trap. He took out his new shotgun.

A SPAS-12, the weapon had represented more of an indulgence than a precaution when he bought it. A good slide-action shotgun would have been enough. Instead, he bought the SPAS, a 12-gauge assault weapon with dual automatic-manual action modes. Fitted with an Aimpoint site, the weapon cost almost a thousand dollars total, including gunsmithing. But he could afford it. And what it did to beer cans made him laugh all day.

He gripped the cold plastic and phosphate-black steel. His right index finger confirmed the position of the safety. Then he went to the guest room. "Julie," he hissed. He listened for sounds from the front of the house as he waited for her answer. "Julie!"

"He'll be quiet in a minute, dad. Sorry he woke you up."

"Call the police right now."

"What?"

"Don't talk. Call the police. Tell them—"

Glass shattered.

2

Waves broke in the night. The cool predawn wind flagged the motel's curtains. Listening to the surf and the distant sounds of the Pacific Coast Highway, Carl Lyons held Flor Trujillo.

For a few minutes of peace, Lyons floated in the soft darkness of ecstasy, without thought, without memory, without horror or rage. Conscious only of sensation, he heard his breathing and Flor's breathing and the waves breaking on Malibu Beach in one sound, as if the darkness outside of him and the darkness within breathed in one rhythm.

The sensation flowered and became a mosaic of perceptions: the warmth of Flor's thigh against his face, the throb of her femoral artery, the caress of her hand on his leg. He felt the breeze on his sweat.

Sensations without thought. Sensations defining the form of his body, where his body touched Flor, where his body touched the wadded and tangled sheets of the bed, where the night wind touched him. For minutes, he existed only as a form defined by sensations.

Then he remembered their pleasure. The sweat-slick flesh of Flor's thighs, his fingers clawing into her flesh, her muscles snapping taut like steel cables as she spasmed in ecstasy, her cries and gasps, his breathing locked with hers. The rhythm and tempo had intoxicated them, her arms gripping him, pulling him against her as if urging him to plunge deeper into her, to thrust deep into the center of her self, her hands jerking him against her, and then his climax.

Her tongue touched him again, the spin of her tongue stopping his memories. He groaned and moved in the bed. "Oh . . . no. Can't."

"Let's make it number five."

"Five?"

"Four so far."

"Impossible. . . ."

"What?"

"This is amazing."

"We're just discharging. It's two months since that time in Washington."

Lyons thought back. Washington. Flor had flown into Dulles and called him at Stony Man. They had an evening and most of the night before his pager buzzed with a call from Stony Man. He flew to Guatemala, she flew to Colombia. He traveled as a soldier, she as a courier. They both fought. He felt his identity returning, the fears and hatreds and horrible, shuddering memories rushing into the pleasure-drained void of his mind, like a flight of bats crowding through the eye sockets of a skull.

"Please don't talk."

"Who wants to talk?" Her legs circled him. She locked her ankles behind him. He smelled the fragrance of her hair. The bed began to squeak and rock. Once again he started to slam into her.

Laughing, she responded to his violence with slow, sensuous writhing of her hips. But after a minute of his body slamming her, she whispered, "Easy. Easy. Slow down. Easy."

He continued slamming her. She told him, "Stop it. Slow down, you're hurting me."

Grabbing her hips in his hands, he continued, not seeking to give or gain but only desperately wanting unconsciousness.

Flor defended herself. Grasping his head in both hands, she pressed her sharp thumbnails against his closed eyes. She put only slight pressure against the eyelids as she warned him, "Stop now!"

Lyons threw himself aside, twisting his face away from the knives of her thumbnails, reflexively straightarming Flor away to a safe distance. His breath came in gasps as he leaned against the headboard.

A siren screamed from the highway, the sound rising and falling, coming closer. The years of service with the LAPD left him with the habit of listening for the identity of the vehicle. Only an ambulance, surely, taking an accident casualty to the hospital?

Or maybe a sheriff's black-and-white racing to

the rescue of a fellow officer? Did an officer at this moment, at this precise moment, hold his guts with one hand while he radioed for help? If Lyons had a scanner he would know. Maybe he could help somehow—

"What's wrong? What's going on with you?" Flor said. "One minute you're a lover and the next, you're...you're berserk."

"Nothing. I just got too rough. I'm sorry."

"No, Carl. I don't mean just now. I mean all night. This afternoon. You're here, then you're not. You're someplace else. You see things. Your face goes hard, like you're ready to attack something. Someone."

"Me? Do that?" He forced a laugh.

"Sometimes you are a scary guy."

Lyons laughed at the understatement. His Able Team partners—Rosario Blancanales and Gadgets Schwarz—also thought of him as a scary guy. "You are five different kinds of scary, scary dude" to quote both Gadgets and the founder of Able Team, Mack Bolan.

"I am," he finally told her, laughing as if he joked. "I am a very scary guy. I even scare myself."

"You may be, but you're a decent man first. A good man. You're easy to like. I liked you before I even really met you. I ever tell you that?"

"What? You don't know anything about me. Not what I do, not who I am or was—"

"Yes, I do. That time in Bolivia. When the Justice Department wanted me to help create an identity for your team. I read your file. And your partners' files. And I wouldn't have you three anywhere near me until I knew everything I could. Simple little things like information and common sense keep me alive. I read and reread your file. In fact, I knew all about you before you even saw me.''

"Is that why you came on to me on the yacht? I mean, that was out of the blue.''

"Why? I thought you'd be a good risk for an affair. And it worked out.''

Lyons laughed. "I feel like a mail-order bride. Dude by dossier. You must have good recommendations. Why'd they let you in on all that information?''

"Why not? I needed to judge your character. Your commander recognized that.''

"What about the rest of it?''

"What?''

"The operations. The missions. What did you think?''

"I didn't get that. I only got your personal files. Nothing about—''

"Oh. Then you don't know.''

"I can guess. Don't forget the time in Miami with your Colonel Phoenix and that Cuban Romeo.''

"I heard about it,'' Lyons nodded. "All you did was drive the car—''

"What? They said that? I just drove the car? I

had to kill two men in Miami, before we even went to the camp. So I just drove the car? That's like saying the kamikaze just flew the plane.''

"I'm joking." Lyons rolled in the bed and held her. "They told me all about it. Very extreme.''

"Was it?''

"You tell me. You were there. I only heard the stories.''

"I mean, was that mission extreme? Or is that what you do all the time?''

Lyons sat up again. He reached out for one of the beers beside the bed. He twisted off the cap and gulped. Foam ran down his face and into his chest hair.

Flor's hand massaged the cold foam over his chest and shoulder. Her fingers traced the rope-like scar where a 7.62 NATO slug had touched his side, breaking ribs and making him cough blood for weeks. Her fingers found other scars where fire or knives or shrapnel had marked his body.

"You don't get scars like these working in an office.''

"I used to be a cop. They'd dispatch us to break up a family fight, and the family would call a truce long enough to beat us half to death.''

"This scar on your arm is new." She touched his left arm where the scabs and discoloration had finally disappeared after months of healing. A crescent-moon scar remained from a wound caused, absurd as it seemed, by a rearview mirror thrown by the impact of a machine-gun slug. The mirror had almost broken his arm.

She traced the new-moon welt with a finger. "Where'd you get it?"

"Playing football on the beach. I fell and—"

"Bullshit."

"Really, I fell down on—"

"A cookie cutter, which just happened to be there."

"Nah, an attack-trained clam. Fell on it and woke it up. Snap!"

"Carl, you joke and you laugh. But it isn't funny to see you. You're haunted. It's like you've got different people moving around inside you. What's happened to you? What have they got you doing?"

"You don't have clearance." He gulped down the last of the beer, twisted the cap off another.

"Are the three of you, the two other men and you, and the others I met— Are you a hit unit?"

"You don't have clearance."

"Are you an assassin?"

Lyons did not answer.

Flor pressed her question. "I do have clearance. The phone call came through last week. I'm detaching from the Drug Enforcement Agency. I'm staying on the agency payroll but I'll be answering to both the agency and your Stony Man. They call me an Interface Operative now. Drugs and terrorism—"

"Oh, God, no. . . ." Lyons groaned. He left the bed, paced the motel room. "Why'd he do this?"

"Who? Who's he? I got the call from the Justice Department."

"Phoenix."

"The colonel?"

"I'll tell you this, without clearance and without 'highest authority.' When you get your check, buy whatever you want. Listen to me. Don't put any money in the bank. Don't buy life insurance. Buy the best clothes, the best shoes. Buy anything that'll give you a laugh."

"It's dangerous. Is that what you're telling me? So you think it's so safe, what I've done? Pretending to be an international dope gangster? Do you want to protect me? You think I will die?"

"Getting killed ain't it. . . ." Lyons pointed to his right eye. "It's what you see. After that, dying, thinking about dying isn't the same. You recognize the advantages of being dead. No memories. No thinking—"

"Where have they sent you? What have you done?"

"You really got clearance? That the truth?"

"They want me to fly back with you. After your demonstration at the academy."

Lyons stood naked in the darkness. He looked around at the walls and furniture, the infinite number of small hiding places for microphones and minitransmitters. He glanced at Flor's purse and folded clothing.

He had rented the room at random. No one—not Flor, not even he himself—knew they would stay ın the Malibu motel. With an afternoon and night to spend together before his demonstration of the Atchisson assault shotgun at the LAPD Academy firing range the next day, he had driven north on the Pacific Coast Highway. He saw the motel sign and stopped. Totally on a whim. Still, he took no chances. . .

As he put on a sweat shirt and swimming trunks, he motioned for Flor to dress. "How about a walk on the beach?"

"You won't talk in here?"

Lyons shook his head.

On the beach, walking arm in arm on the cold sand, he told her of his work in the past year. He talked until sunrise.

Flor listened to all the horror and inhumanity and suffering.

"What do you think?" Lyons concluded. "Is that what you want to do with your life?"

"Those people in New York, in the Amazon, in Guatemala, those Salvadorans—all of them, they're alive because of you. You and Blancanales and Gadgets, right?"

"Yeah, I think about that a lot. That's what makes it all worth it."

"Do you think it would be any different for me? I've seen what you've seen, but I couldn't do anything about it. Now I can. What greater opportunity could I hope for?"

"The terrorists—there's always more. We kill one, a hundred come. We kill the hundred, the

Soviets only open more training camps. There's no end to the killing and suffering.''

"And what if we didn't fight?''

"Take a tour of Cambodia. That could be America. And the Soviets would put Pol Pot in charge of American reeducation.''

"Then we fight. . . .''

Lyons nodded. He put his arms around Flor and held her, the rise and fall of her chest soft against his muscles. He tasted the sweat-salt in her hair as the offshore wind blew strands of it over his face. He closed his eyes to the graying Pacific, the red-streaked skyline of mountains and beach-front homes. He wished he knew the future. But he did not, could not, and would not want to know when the bullet or knife or blastflash would end him.

When he died, he died. But now, in this moment of life and pleasure on Malibu Beach, he held the woman he loved. He thought of nothing but love.

3

Three hours later, at the firing range of the Los Angeles Police Department's Academy in Elysian Park, Lyons paced the walkways. No one had appeared for his demonstration of the Atchisson selective-fire assault shotgun. The firing range remained deserted at nine-thirty in the morning. No academy cadets, no police officers used the range. At nine o'clock, the scheduled time for the demonstration, only Lyons and Flor stood at the long counter running the length of the facility. Now, after they had waited a half hour, none of the invited officers or security personnel had appeared.

Only the steady pop-pop-pop of a Heckler & Koch PSP 9mm pistol broke the silence. With one hand, then the other, Flor put groups of slugs through the black of a fifty-foot target as fast as she could pull the trigger.

Lyons looked back, saw the young woman rehearsing magazine changes with her right and then her left hand.

Struggling with the awkward position of the magazine release on the butt, Flor attempted to somehow release and eject the empty magazine while holding the next magazine in her off hand. Every time, the hand that held the full mag blocked the drop of the spent magazine. Finally she returned the high-tech German autopistol to its shipping box.

The booming of full-powered cartridges reaffirmed her faith in the downscaled Browning design of the Detonics .45 she always carried. Gripping the small pistol in both hands, she rapid-fired six rounds at the fifty-foot target.

Six .45-caliber slugs scored on the target. As she changed magazines, she called out to Lyons, "Perhaps there was a misunderstanding. The wrong day on the announcement. Perhaps that."

"I typed the announcements myself. I had friends call me long distance to say they'd show up. This is much too weird. At least there should be guys here doing their monthly qualifying. I'm going to call some people."

Jogging down the brick-walled drive, he glanced across the fountain plaza to the city-operated restaurant. In Lyons's years of city service, police and maintenance personnel had crowded the cafeteria for breakfast. Not today. Only one Mechanical Department truck parked at the curb. He went to the guard post manned by an academy cadet.

"What's going on?" Lyons asked him. "Someone declare today a holiday?"

The young Chicano woman looked at him oddly. "Everyone's out there. Looking for them."

"What? Who're they looking for? What's happened?"

"You don't have a television? You don't read the papers?" She turned over a newspaper on her desk. Lyons read the bold headline:

NIGHT OF HORROR
Mass Slayings, Gang Atrocities

FLOR STAYED AT THE WHEEL of their rented car while Lyons went to the pay phone near the entry of Parker Center, the main administrative offices for the Los Angeles Police Department. He dialed the number of a longtime friend and partner.

"Detective Towers," a voice answered.

"Hey, Bill. It's a crazy Federal you know."

"You hotshots don't waste any time. Who called you?"

"No one. Remember the demonstration? At the academy—"

"Oh, yeah. Sorry. Forgot all about it. This shit, you know."

"Yeah, I know. I bought a newspaper. Shit is right. Very bad shit. What's the story?"

"This an official call or what? If it isn't, the policy is that I can't talk to you."

"I'm officially calling as a concerned citizen. From the pay phone outside the front door."

"I'm sorry, but the department cannot comment on this case to any civilians or outside law-enforcement agency. If you are patient, I'm sure the newspapers will carry every detail of the investigation, arrest and eventual acquittal of all the low-life scum punks involved. Three minutes, okay?''

"I thought you could fill me in."

"Absolutely not, sir. Goodbye."

Lyons waited at the steps until Bill Towers walked from the building. Without greeting his friend, Lyons rushed to the street. Lyons motioned with his right hand as he watched the traffic for the rental car. Flor turned the corner. Lyons looked to his right. Towers hurried away.

"You talk to your friend?" Flor asked as Lyons got in.

"Don't take off just yet. Let him make some distance."

"He's up there?"

"In the checkered sports coat."

Flor laughed. "That coat! Where do cops get their clothes?"

"He's got kids in college. He thinks they're more important than how he looks. Go. He'll be waiting around the corner."

Accelerating into traffic, Flor braked at a crosswalk. City workers crossed the street. Several read newspapers with headlines that screamed:

NIGHT OF HORROR

GANG TERROR

RACIAL OVERTONES TO CRIMES

A group of professionals argued among themselves, the voices of the well-dressed and immaculately groomed managers and attorneys loud even in the noise of the cars and trucks.

"This will unleash the worst police repression since the sixties—"

"The department will just dress the Triple K in blue and send them out to kill everything that isn't white—"

Music blasted away the traffic noise. Three teenagers in sneakers and torn jeans and identical black nylon jackets—despite the midmorning heat—wove into the crowd. One of the punks carried an expensive "ghetto blaster." The professionals looked up to see the ghetto punks.

The argument stopped. The professionals quietly scattered. The punks looked around at the fearful people and laughed. The light changed to green. Ignoring the crosswalk's signal, the punks strolled in front of the waiting cars. When cars attempted to proceed, one punk pointed a pistol-finger at the drivers. The cars stopped. The punks bebopped in front of Flor and Lyons.

One punk saw Flor. He stared at the beautiful young Hispanic woman sitting with the Anglo man. He grinned, showing all his yellow and broken teeth. Stroking the crotch of his filthy blue jeans, he swaggered up to Flor's window. "Hey, baby. Wanna get high with a cool brother—"

Flor jammed the muzzle of her Detonics .45 into the punk's mouth.

Spitting teeth and blood, the punk staggered

backward into slow-moving traffic. A truck's fender hit him, bounced him into the car waiting behind Flor and Lyons. The truck did not stop.

Accelerating away, Flor laughed. Lyons returned his Colt Python to his shoulder holster and looked back.

The punk crawled on the asphalt, screaming and cursing, blood spraying from his lips. No one stopped to help him. His friends stood on the curb while traffic swerved around him without slowing.

Turning right, Flor stopped in front of Detective Towers. The middle-aged policeman with twenty years of worry lining his face glanced around at the people on the sidewalk before swinging open the back door. In a second, they merged with traffic again.

When he saw Flor, Towers blinked. He studied her for a moment before asking Lyons, "Who is your assistant?"

"My name is Flor. Carl, wipe this off." She passed the Detonics to Lyons. He turned and grinned to his old friend.

"Should have seen what just happened!" Lyons used a rental-company brochure to wipe saliva from the muzzle of the autopistol. "This punk thought he'd abuse the pretty lady. Turned out he got a forty-five in the mouth."

"You shot someone? On the street there?" Towers looked back.

"No shooting." Lyons used his thumbnail to scrape a bit of flesh out of the hairline space between the Detonics's slide and the frame. "Just low-velocity steel."

Towers laughed. He ran his hand through his thinning hair and reached inside his coat for his cigarettes. He tapped one out of the pack. He counted the cigarettes remaining and then put the cigarette back.

"Glad you showed up, hardman. This man needs some laughs. You read the newspapers?"

"Can't be true."

"It's worse." The detective stared out at the parking lots and shop fronts. The heat and midmorning smog created a gray day without colors or horizons. The boulevards faded into the near distance, the buildings and cars becoming only shadows within the gray.

"Much worse. I thought Manson was the ultimate. But these punks, these gangs made Charlie and his little girls look like Bo Peep and the sheep. You two work together?"

"Flor's coming in as. . . what did you call it?"

"We can talk?" Flor questioned Lyons before she answered.

"Bill was in on the Hydra op," Lyons said. "He knows enough to be a superstar at any congressional hearing. But only about Los Angeles."

"I'll be an interface between the DEA and his group," she said. "The terrorists seem to be funding their forces with dope money. Follow the dope, find the terrorists. Follow the terrorists, find the dope. It is natural that I work with Carl."

"There's drugs in this. The punks were up on some crazy drug."

"Was it PCP?" Lyons asked.

"Back where the gang went up against the old man with the shotgun, one of our men found some drug. And you know, he gave it the sniff test. Instant freak-out. His partners had to knock him down and tie his arms and legs. He's in the psycho ward right now."

"What was it?"

"Isn't Angel Dust. It's something else. Soon as you drop me off, I'm getting on the phone to the chief. I'm requesting very special federal assistance. Then maybe you two can come on as liaison.

"Because we're going to need you. This stuff the gangs got, what those gangs did to those college girls, what they did to that Mexican family, human beings can't do that. I think it's the drug. Doctors don't know what it is. Chemists don't know.

"And all I know is what it does. That dope. . . . It's got to be something straight out of hell."

4

When Lyons called Stony Man from a scrambler-fitted pay phone in Philippe's French Dip Sandwich Café, April Rose switched him directly to Hal Brognola.

"Finally, you called in," the cigar-smoking big Fed said. "We got a job for you out there in Los Angeles."

"The crazy dope?"

"What?"

"The gangs that have gone berserk on some kind of super-PCP out here. I want in on the action."

"If you'll listen, I'll give you your assignment. It's related. There was a weapon found on one of the punks who got killed. A Colt Automatic Rifle, one of those abbreviated M-16s—"

"High-class weapon for a gang punk."

"Let me give you details. The CAR was an old one. Made in 1965. No bolt assist—"

"An XM-177E1? That's obsolete. A collector's item. Where'd they get that?"

"That's the question. Let me continue, Carl, please. The serial number had been ground off, but the FBI got a latent impression with X-ray macrophotography. We know where it came from. Vietnam. And you have to find out how the gang got it. Then we'll trace it back from there.''

''What about Political and the Wizard?''

''They're packing now. They'll be on their way this afternoon.''

''So they'll be here tonight, my time. And Flor Trujillo. Can she get in on this?''

''She out there? We called the DEA. They said she had the week off. If she wants the assignment, she can check the drug angle. But the source of that weapon is the number-one priority.''

''What's her clearance? She told me we have some kind of interface arrangement in the works.''

''That's the official term.''

''But what's it mean?''

''Improvise. We never employed an 'interface' agent before. It's a gray area. But keep your personal relationship out of it, understand?''

''Don't know what you're talking about, Hal.''

The Fed laughed. ''Everybody else does.''

''What does everyone else know? What's the gossip?''

''The details of your personal life go in your file. Along with your biography, your qualifications, your mission debriefings—it's our business to know everything about you. And about Miss Trujillo. And what we know about you two so far satisfies all our security criteria.''

"So she's cleared?''

"You can talk with her.''

"And what's her authorization?''

"There's the gray area. If she's working in liaison with your Team, she shares whatever authorization your Team has. If she's alone, she's subject to Drug Enforcement Agency procedures and regulations. Unless Stony Man has issued the mission directive. Then she has whatever authorization the mission carries.''

"But she's with us on this one?''

"If she wants it. Looks like a straightforward PCP case to me.''

"It isn't. I talked with a friend on the force. It's something new.''

"It's a fact that Los Angeles gets all the new drugs first. But it isn't up to Stony Man to apprehend every garage chemist in the country.''

"The police chemists and the university labs can't break the formula. And if they can't break it, how can some low-life doper make it?''

"Put Miss Trujillo to work. Perhaps she can answer that.''

"So we've got official authorization now?''

"Highest. But be discreet, understand? We don't want to see you on the eleven o'clock news.''

"Yes, sir. Not me, sir. Over and out, sir.''

Crossing the sawdust-carpeted dining room, Lyons smiled at Flor. He saw that she had bought a stack of newspapers while he talked on the phone. She read an Extra printed in red ink on an international socialist publication. The nameplate at the top of the page bore a radiant red star flanked by the portraits of Vladimir Lenin and Joseph Stalin.

"Where'd you get that shit?"

"A newsstand."

"Only in America," Lyons commented as he pulled a stool to the wide linoleum-covered table.

"Listen to what they're writing." Flor read aloud from a front-page editorial. " 'Fascist Pig Junta Unleashed. In a mobilization and mass strike equaled only by the Nazi blitzkrieg of 1939, the self-described protectors of Los Angeles struck at defenseless black and brown families throughout Southern California. Elite SWAT teams and blue-uniformed storm troopers dragged innocent teenagers from their beds in coordinated predawn kidnappings...observers report torture...trucks crowded with chained and gagged teenagers departed for concentration camps—' "

"Stop!" Lyons hissed. "Stop talking that shit!"

Flor laughed. Lyons's anger faded as he watched her laugh, his eyes marveling at the smooth line of her throat, the perfect café-au-lait color of her flesh, the red-as-blood lip gloss she wore. Her thin eyebrows, startling lines of black above her black eyes, feathered away without makeup or artificial shaping. She wore her hair tied back this morning, the smooth flow of her forehead and hair emphasizing the Andean blade of her nose. So beautiful, so deadly.

"Did your boss say he would accept this woman?" Flor touched the center of her café-au-lait chest. "Does he think I am qualified?"

Deadly. Lyons thought of Flor Trujillo as deadly. She stood five feet eight in her highest heels. At approximately one hundred twenty-five pounds, she appeared very slim despite her strength and conditioning. Naturally quick, training and self-discipline and ideological motivation made her a dangerous opponent to anyone on earth.

Deadly, his mind repeated. He had seen men twice her weight and inconceivably murderous reduced to smears of blood and bone fragments before they could raise a weapon in defense.

He had the urge to lie to her. To tell her Stony Man had rejected her. That her foreign birth made her an unacceptable security risk. And why not another lie? That he had resigned in protest. No more killing. No more blood and horror.

He wanted to walk away from her. Get in the rented car and floor it. Follow a compass bearing away from this terrorized city. A city defended by men and women who could not even expect the respect of the citizens. Who had to hide their careers from their neighbors. Why should he continue? Why should he risk this woman? Why should he risk his love in a nightmare world of high-velocity mutilation?

"Don't just make moon eyes at me," she whispered. "What did your Colonel Phoenix say?"

He told the truth. "We're in it."

5

A puzzle of human parts lay on the fiberglass slab. As morgue attendants and pathologists worked at other tables, Detective Towers identified the mixed limbs and organs to Lyons and Flor.

"That's two girls. Found them in the same bedroom. They and these others came from the sorority house...."

Lyons glanced at the hacked corpses, looked away. He had seen it all before. Flor had not. She stared, her face slack with incomprehension. She seemed transfixed by the horror.

Towers continued along the aisle, pointing to each table as he walked through the morgue. "This is the Valencia family. Punks got them on the freeway. There was a baby, too. But it's not here. What could be scraped off the freeway, the pathologists sent straight through to cremation. And down here's some punks. What kind of shotgun did you plan to demonstrate out at the range?"

"An Atchisson...."

"Here's a demonstration of a SPAS-12. What do you think?"

Five naked teenagers lay on tables. Old knife

scars and jailhouse tattoos marked their bodies. Two had feet mangled by blasts of birdshot. Blasts to their chests had killed them. A third teenager showed a hideous wound to his ribs, which had also torn away his right biceps. A point-blank shot to the center of his chest had killed him. The other two had lost their heads.

"Very effective. But an Atchisson has a box magazine," Lyons said. "Whoever shot these shits ended up with an empty weapon. Count the hits. Eight shots. Maybe he had a round in the chamber. That would've been nine rounds. Against five punks. What if they'd been six?"

"You want the story on what happened?"

"That's why I'm here."

"Look at their hands and legs. See the cuts? They smashed through a plate-glass window. The cuts didn't slow them down."

Lyons picked up one teenager's arm and examined a line of welted scar tissue on his forearm and inner elbow area. "This one was an addict. Maybe he didn't feel it."

"Maybe not. The old man told them to stop. I tell you, that old guy had nerve. He turned on the porch and entry lights by remote control. That silhouetted all of them. He waited until they shot back before cutting loose. He shot the first two in the feet. Didn't stop them. Those punks just ripped the house up with pistols and those automatic rifles. The old man gets hurt, but he holds his ground. Finally, he got them all. They wouldn't stop. He said they kept screaming, 'Die, whitey! Die, whitey!' The ones with the ripped-up feet, they walked on the stumps. The one with the ripped arm, he took the weapon in his left hand and rushed the old man. After that, he didn't mess around. He put his fancy laser sight—one of those Aimpoints—on their heads and he put them out. How's that for a horror story?''

"Horror story? This little scum fest had a happy ending. What if he'd only had a .38 Special?''

"You're a real cheery guy, you know that, Carl? I mean, people might think you're not a lover of mankind.''

"I love people! But not everyone loves me. That's why I carry a Colt Python. For special occasions, I carry the Python and a .45 and my Atchisson. Now was this the gang with the drug?''

Towers nodded. "That's another story. We'll go talk to the doctors.''

Turning to call Flor, Lyons saw the young Hispanic woman staring at the murdered Valencias: the shotgun-blasted Raoul, the raped-and-hacked Maria, the stabbed-and-shot young boys. Swaying slightly on her feet, she grabbed the edge of an examining table to steady herself.

Lyons went to her and held her. Her breath caught, then steadied as she stopped a sob. As Lyons held her, he saw her tears fall onto the polished fiberglass of the examining table, the tears beading to sparkling jewels of sorrow.

A UNIFORMED SERGEANT stood in the waiting room of Intensive Care, guarding the entry to the ward. Towers showed his identification to the officer.

"And who are they?" the sergeant demanded.

"Federals."

"I'll have to call for a clearance before they can go in." The sergeant reached for an interhouse phone.

Lyons shook his head. "We don't have to see the man. All we want is information. Could a doctor come out to brief us?"

"I'll call for an okay," the sergeant told him.

As the sergeant talked on the phone, Lyons asked Towers, "We are on the same side, aren't we?"

"Usually," Towers answered. "Of course, if I told who you really are—" the graying, balding detective glanced to both sides; no one could hear his words "—he'd call for his mama."

"What are you talking about?" Lyons demanded. "Cops don't have mothers. They make us at Smith & Wesson."

"A doctor's on the way," the sergeant told them.

Towers whispered again. "He knows!"

Flor, still pale and silent from the horror of the morgue, watched the ex-partners joking with one another. Towers pronounced in a low voice, "Today, in recognition of years of dedication to public service in Los Angeles and the world, Los Angeles police officers ended the career of Carl Lyons, ex-

police officer, ex-detective, ex-specialist in coun-
terterrorism, with a quick hypo of Thorazine and
the award of a Kevlar straitjacket. Yes, ladies and
gentlemen, you are now safe from this madman,
who thought he could make a difference. Said his
longtime friend and compatriot in the self-
righteous nonsense of criminal suppression, Detective Bill Towers, 'I'm moving to the Arctic Circle.'
'Why do that?' this announcer asked. Detective
Towers, a twenty-year veteran of futile opposition
to the People's Liberation Mob of San Quentin,
said, 'I heard you can train polar bears to eat
creeps.'"

Shouts outside the waiting room announced two
long-haired and bearded news technicians. One
carried a shoulder-slung tape recorder and six-
foot-long boom microphone. The other carried a
small video camera and portable video recorder.

The cameraman flicked on the video recorder's
power and put the camera to his shoulder. Turning his back, Lyons grabbed Flor. He put his arm
around her shoulder and drew her near. In the reflection of a blacked-out window in the door of
Intensive Care, Lyons watched as Towers rushed
at the cameraman.

Three men, two hospital administrators in light
blue jackets and a slight wavy-haired man in a cor-
duroy casual suit, crowded through the waiting-
room entry. The administrators attempted to
block the door, but the third man, protesting in a
nasal shriek, pressed through. "Continue this

harassment of the press and you can expect to see me in court! Do you understand me? The truth must be told! You cannot restrain the free expression of the truth!''

Towers held up his hands to block the lens. But the cameraman swiveled in another direction. Focusing the zoom lens, the cameraman video-recorded the commentator's shrill protests and gestures. Towers rushed past the technicians. The sound man put the microphone over the three men.

The commentator faced the camera. ''This is Mark Lannon outside the Intensive Care Ward of USC Medical Center, where the Los Angeles Police Department holds incommunicado one of the officers responsible for the slaughter of five young brown and black teenagers who committed the crime of entering a white neighborhood.''

At the entry to the waiting room, Towers took a fingernail-trim set from his pocket. He jammed the nail file into the keyed light switch.

The high-pitched voice of Mark Lannon continued. ''Witnesses to the atrocity report the officer went mad with blood lust and attacked his partners in murder. The Los Angeles Police Department refuses to confirm or contradict the statements of on-the-spot witnesses. However, this reporter has gained additional information on the incident—''

The lights went out in the windowless room. In total darkness, Lannon's voice protested. ''This is deliberate! This is criminal harassment of the press! This is fascist suppression— Ugh. . . . ''

His voice cut off as a fist slapped skin. Metal crashed. Someone screamed in pain as fists beat flesh. A penlight revealed the form of the cameraman on the floor. A leg wearing gray cotton-polyester and a soft leather neoprene shoe—the color of the slacks Lyons wore and the style of shoe he preferred—place-kicked the video camera into the air. The light flicked out. Plastic shattered as a heel crashed down again and again. The light flashed on again to reveal the smashed video recorder. A hand tore a videocassette from the destroyed machine.

From the side of the room came the sound of glass breaking. Another shriek tore the darkness. The penlight beam showed a hand lifting the sound man from the floor by his beard. A knee in gray slacks crushed his nose.

The door to the Intensive Care Ward opened, light flooding the waiting room. In a blur of indistinct motion, several forms rushed into the ward. Others rushed out the other door.

At the waiting room entry, one of the administrators rekeyed the light switch, then continued out to the corridor.

Alone in the waiting room, surrounded by smashed equipment, Mark Lannon and his technicians groaned on the floor.

Lyons and Towers and Flor glanced back through the ward door as it closed.

"You just met the correspondents from our local Communist news station," Towers told Lyons and Flor.

"Wonder what those Commies are doing on the floor?" Lyons asked. "Think it's a public orgy?"

The uniformed sergeant laughed first. Then four officers and ex-officers all shared a long laugh.

A doctor watched for a moment before asking, "What happened out there?"

Lyons turned to the doctor. "The lights went out and...I think they fell down, but I don't know...."

"We were so busy getting in here," Towers added. "Didn't see what happened...."

"Who wanted to talk about the officer?"

Their laughter stopped.

"What's his condition?" Towers asked.

"He'll be staying for observation, but we think he's improving. We tried the standard sedative and antipsychotic drugs but finally we resorted to the expediency of changing his blood, which proved to be helpful."

"You changed his blood?"

"Then we upped the antipsychotics until his convulsions and rages stopped. Drastic, but the treatment seems effective. The residual amounts may trigger repeated seizures. I believe the continuing treatment will be rest and calm until we can identify the chemical that initiated his attacks. Then we can attempt to neutralize whatever traces of the chemical remain in his body."

"Have any idea what the drug was?" Lyons asked.

"A drug? I don't know that this chemical is a drug. It seems to activate areas of the brain usually unaffected by drugs. It creates rages. Like a drug, it makes the individual unaware of pain, but that may be a side effect of the rage. The police department's chemists already have a sample," the doctor said. He was enthusiastic. "And we've sent pathologists to the morgue to take samples of the five teenagers' brains. I'm really quite excited about this. I've already outlined a paper I plan to publish. This is all very, very extraordinary."

Lyons nodded. "Yeah, it sure is."

ON ANOTHER FLOOR OF THE HOSPITAL, in a private room guarded by an LAPD officer in the white uniform of a nurse, Lou Stevens rested after minor surgery. The white-uniformed woman—an officer with black-belt degrees in both karate and judo—admitted Towers, Lyons and Flor after they presented their identification.

"He's awake," she whispered before opening the door. "He wants to talk. He's very shook up by what happened."

"No doubt," Towers answered. He knocked before opening the door.

In the sun-bright white room, Lou Stevens sat up in the cranked-up hospital bed. Newspapers with bold headlines covered the blanket. He looked up from reading as they entered.

"Mr. Stevens, how are you?" Towers shook hands with the white-haired electrical engineer. "Doctor told me you didn't even need general anesthesia."

"I don't even need to be in the hospital. The bullet went through the wall before it hit me. Doctor showed me the fragments he took out of my leg. I got bigger pieces of metal than that still in me from the Philippines."

"World War II?" Towers asked.

"Signal Corps."

"Is that how you got your start in electronics?"

"Electronics?" Stevens laughed. "That's what I thought. Wanted to go to trade school or college, but I didn't think I'd ever have that much time or money. So I enlisted. Thought I'd do a four-year course in the Army, learning about radios. What I did was unroll wire for field telephones while everybody shot at me. Japs thought I was a soldier. Our side thought I was a Jap infiltrator. Soon enough I learned to dig with my nose while I ran with my legs. Sort of a human plow. Except never more than three inches off the ground. Something like a torpedo through the dirt."

All of them laughed. Towers took the opportunity to introduce Lyons and Flor. "This is my friend Carl Stone. He's with federal law enforcement. And Angelica Lopez. She's Federal, also. They'd like to talk to you about what happened last night."

Stevens tapped one of the newspaper stories.

"I'll tell you. It was awful. But what I see in the papers.... I had my daughter and her husband in the next room. My month-old grandson. I gave those...those...delinquents a chance. I told them. And they started shooting. That machine gun they had, it just ripped the place apart. So I shot the first two in the feet. But good God, they didn't stop...."

"Did they seem to feel the pain?" Lyons asked gently.

"They started screaming, but...but they only really screamed when I told them to get out. They screamed, but it wasn't...it wasn't like pain. 'Die, whitey, die, you white....' They used words I won't repeat in the presence of a young lady. I shot the first two in the feet and they went down. The one with the machine gun started shooting everywhere. So I shot him. The ones with pistols saw me and shot. That's when I got wounded. I fell down.

"They rushed me with those pistols. I was on the floor, and I put the little red dot right on their faces. Shot them.

"Goddamn glad for all the time I've spent on the range shooting skeet. Those two fall down, and I see the one on the ground trying to get that little machine gun. He's wounded and bleeding like...like...like terrible casualties I saw in the Philippines. But he's still trying to get the machine gun. I had to shoot him.

"And the other two. One of them, his foot is

gone. And he stands up and tries to run at me. Not away. At me, with a machete. 'Die, whitey,' he screamed. I shot him. The other one, he takes a pistol off the floor. I shot him, too.''

For a moment, the grandfather stared into space. He shook his head at the remembered images. ''It was so awful. It was so goddamn awful.''

Lyons put his hand on Stevens's shoulder. ''You saved your family. Those punks weren't there to steal. They were completely doped out of their minds and looking to kill.''

''I know, I know. But I'll never be able to forget what . . . what I had to do.''

Towers spoke then. ''Sir, you gave us the only break we've had so far. We've got a start on that crazy drug, and we've got the weapon and the bodies. Without that, we'd have nothing to work on. It's a start. You can be proud of that.''

''Thanks for trying to cheer me up, but I've got to live with it. I'll see what I did for the rest of my life. I'll never forget.''

A knock sounded on the door. Towers glanced to Lyons and Flor. The two Federals turned their backs to the door. Towers asked, ''Who's there?''

''Urgent message for Mr. Lou Stevens!''

''He's resting,'' Towers answered.

''Who's the message from?'' Stevens called out.

''I don't know, sir. I'm only a messenger.''

''Bring it in,'' Stevens told the unseen messenger.

"I'll get it," Towers said.

But before the detective could go to the door, a young Chicano man dressed in a suit and tie stepped across the small hospital room. The messenger slapped an envelope down on the bed. "You're served! You'll pay for murdering those brothers!"

Towers recognized the messenger. "You're one of the Youth Action lawyers. They let you in!"

Lyons started for the messenger. "What do you mean, he's served? Is that a lawsuit? For what?"

Towers shoved him back. Now the detective demanded, "What is that?"

As he went out the door, the lawyer turned and announced, "See you in court, you racist butcher!"

6

In 1969, a group of North American and Chicano social activists created the Los Angeles Youth Action Committee. Veterans of marches and riots against the undeclared Asian war, the activists had rejected the violence and fugitive existence of the more radical elements of the youthful counterculture. Unlike the Weatherman and the Black Panthers, the activists believed they could achieve greater social change through alliance with the progressive elements of their government.

They opened a storefront office in downtown Los Angeles. Though the faces and names changed as the activists returned to college or went to work or traveled the world, the committee never lacked idealistic volunteers for their programs of antidraft counseling, youth guidance, English instruction and Chicano-Native American history.

However, government programs—local, state, federal—never granted the committee the funding necessary to pay salaries. The committee survived on money solicited from students and local merchants to pay rent and office expenses. Fund-raising events provided money for the purchase of typewriters and public-address systems. Month after month, the committee struggled for every dollar as they delivered services to the poor and disadvantaged of Los Angeles.

Then Mario Silva joined the committee. A young second-generation Cuban American—his family had come to the United States when his father, a personal friend of President Batista of Cuba, fled with the deposed general when that nation fell to Fidel Castro—Silva had been graduated from the University of California at Los Angeles in 1969. Though his liberal ideals conflicted with his family's conservative heritage, his father supported him throughout his university years. And the day after Mario passed the State of California Bar Exam his father presented him with an American Express credit card and an around-the-world airline ticket.

To his parents' surprise, after almost a year of travels through Central and South America, Africa and Asia, their son did not talk of his adventures. He did not show them photos or souvenirs purchased in the distant cities of the world. He returned changed, but silent. They would not have known he'd traveled at all except for the many postcards they received, and the year-long accumulation of American Express charges at exclusive hotels, expensive restaurants and auto-rental agencies around the world.

But his work with the Los Angeles Youth Action Committee suggested a compassionate transformation. Throughout his years as a student, he'd demonstrated an ability to master difficult subjects through intense periods of study—total immersion. He broke his discipline only to strut through the ranks of the young women in the college. This reassured his Hispanic father of his son's virility. The senior Silva had once carried a listing of Cuban and North American showgirls eager to advance their careers through "association" with a high-ranking Batista cabinet official. Silva could not imagine his son's not following in his Don Juan rhythms of lust and jilt, infidelity and jealousy.

As a young lawyer volunteering his services to the committee, Mario Silva continued in his discipline of intense work and quick romances. He also worked as a junior associate in the corporate law office of one of his father's friends from pre-Revolutionary Cuba. Often he left the law firm's elegant Wilshire Boulevard offices and drove directly to the dingy, crowded office of the committee to review immigration cases and the marijuana arrests of barrio "homeboys." In the late evenings, he dated young women from the law offices, speeding over the freeways from disco to disco in his Porsche.

Though he did not talk of his volunteer work, his investment of time and choice of cases told of his social concerns. At the expense of his practice of prestigious and lucrative corporate law, he spent hours every evening and weekend with the troubles of illegal aliens and teenage gang boys, poor Chicano families and minimum-wage workers wronged by their employers. His quiet dedication demonstrated what other activists only preached.

His commitment to social causes won the recognition of the other volunteers. A relationship with an attractive young Marxist novelist—she taught classes in English as a Second Language in the evening—assured an inside position with the leadership group despite his links with corporations and antisocialist Cubans. When his Marxist girl friend nominated him, her activist associates honored Mario Silva with the chairmanship of the committee.

As his first move as chairman, he proposed dissolving the committee and the restructuring of their organization as a nonprofit community-service corporation. He surprised his associates with a prepared book-thick proposal detailing the advantages and opportunities of operating a nonprofit corporation within a corporate capitalist society.

With the help of his law firm, Silva created the Los Angeles Youth Action Corporation. With secret aid from his family—strong supporters of President Richard Nixon—LAYAC contributed thousands of dollars to the Committee to Reelect the President. LAYAC organized hundreds of Hispanic youths to encourage registration of voters and knock on doors for the reelection of Richard Nixon.

After the inauguration, LAYAC received a grant of one million dollars from the reelected administration.

With the mandate of offering employment and services for the young people of Los Angeles, Silva invested the money in offices, staff and equipment. He also contributed some of the federal money to the campaigns of local and state leaders.

Merchants and businessmen and corporations found LAYAC particularly useful. When contractors needed ethnic faces and names to satisfy government requirements for minority participation in public projects, Silva established corporate subsidiaries headed by Chicanos or blacks. When national corporations wanted to demonstrate equal-opportunity policies, Silva financed franchises that were owned, managed and staffed by minorities. When manufacturers wanted to establish credibility as progressive employers, Silva gathered hundreds of unemployed teenagers and organized showcase job-training programs for the cameras of newsmen and journalists.

The joint ventures and the media events won the attention of politicians. They recognized flair and success. In the next few years, Silva and the Los Angeles Youth Action Corporation received ten million dollars in federal and state grants, Small Business Administration low-interest loans and private donations. In turn, Silva invested millions in the campaigns of his political friends.

To fully exploit his national connections, Silva created a real-estate subsidiary, which then bought a $500,000 condominium in Washington, D.C. He flew often to the capital to entertain legislators, administrators and foreign political and business leaders.

During the Nixon and Ford administrations, LAYAC expanded far beyond Los Angeles. Ventures in Central America and South America, Europe and the Middle East generated cash flow to the charitable organization. Though the subsidiaries did not show great profits, Silva told his associates he foresaw long-term dividends.

A calculated and cynical observation prompted Silva to decline to offer his staff and volunteers to the campaign to reelect President Ford. Silva knew Ford would lose. The LAYAC volunteers walked the precincts for Carter.

Though the Carter administration sent accountants to review the nonprofit corporation's records and charitable procedures, the federal investigators never actually entered the LAYAC offices. They visited Silva's luxury home in Bel Air to interview the selfless young entrepreneur and glance through a few volumes he had assembled for their reading.

Later, Silva received an award from the Carter administration for his charitable contributions to the underprivileged of Los Angeles and the United States.

Years later, another investigation followed an unfortunate and never-publicized incident involving terrorism. A joint task force of FBI, LAPD and "unknown" commandos found a group of terrorists in a garage financed with LAYAC funds. Though a vicious firefight exterminated the terrorists before they could spray thousands of gallons of binary nerve gas into the night sky of Los Angeles, the incident prompted a thorough check of the garage owner's links to LAYAC. Somehow, Silva learned of the probe and petitioned all his elected friends to support his plea of total ignorance and innocence.

Despite many coincidences and questionable links—LAYAC trucking subsidiaries in Mexico and Central America that might have carried the fifty-gallon drums of binary gas, dead terrorists who had been gang punks in LAYAC counseling programs and the fact that all LAYAC staff personnel and their families had been in San Francisco the night of the planned annihilation of Los Angeles—the federal investigators reported that they had no suspicion of Silva's involvement in the attempted mass murder of the city's people.

That investigation still made Silva's hands shake when he thought of it. His girl friends had noticed that he drank more, often lapsing into the silence of alcohol introspection.

In those times, he questioned the wisdom of his

secret life. He had many fears. If his father knew the truth of his son's success and prosperity, he would murder his son. If the federal government learned the identity of the nation and the organization that sponsored LAYAC, Silva would spend the rest of his life in prison, or with the good luck of escape, exile. If the police learned of his role in the gangs' bloody rampages, Silva faced Death Row.

Silva thought back on the innumerable stories of corruption and easy millions his father told of the Batista regime, when the Silva family enjoyed the prestige of government position and the wealth flowing upward from the hotels and casinos and brothels of Havana. He had also heard the stories of the politics and secret deals necessary to win profits for American corporations. In the United States—his father an ex-fascist colonel, now a corporate attorney—he had become wealthy through the same corrupt techniques he had practiced in pre-Revolutionary Cuba.

Was young Silva to blame for seeking the same advantages?

His university education in business management and his law school's basic courses in tax law revealed to him the difficulties of legally gained success.

Therefore, he looked around him for opportunity. How could a twenty-three-year-old university graduate gain immediate entry into the world of high finance and polite corruption? With his father's law firm? Perhaps after ten years of faithful association, his father and his office partners might grant their junior partner a favor. In other firms? No.

Mario Silva crafted his own plan for immediate wealth. And he did as his father had done; he sold the plan to the general who ruled Cuba.

In his world travels, young Silva never went farther than Cuba. He presented his plan to the Cuban Dirección General de Inteligencia (DGI) and their KGB advisors. When they accepted it, he then stayed the year in their military and intelligence schools while Cuban agents traveled the world with his American Express card, lavishing the wealth of the *gusano* colonel on hotels and restaurants and tourist trinkets to prove that Mario Silva visited those foreign countries.

After his training, Silva returned to Los Angeles and did exactly as he had promised. With Communist dollars, he converted a charitable group to a secret Communist organization. He traveled the world expanding the Los Angeles Youth Action Corporation into a multinational conglomerate of companies. Each company—trucking operations in Mexico and Central America, airlines in the United States, real-estate partnerships in several North American cities—provided services to the Cuban DGI.

Silva's family provided money; LAYAC's many concerns sometimes provided profits. But the Cuban funds ensured success.

On the afternoon after the hideous wave of murders by psychopathic gang punks, Mario Silva paced in front of his wide-screen television, a tall glass of bourbon and ice chilling his hand as he watched the "alternative" evening news.

Broadcast by KMRX—pronounced K-Marx by the station screen personalities—the "alternative news" often featured videotape from Cuba, the Soviet Union and other "peace-loving nations." The station covered every radical community event, specializing in protests against police shootings and crowds of welfare recipients demanding increased benefits. Often K-Marx featured the accomplishments of LAYAC.

And tonight Silva waited for another civil-rights media coup to be announced. The station did not disappoint him. A young blond woman with a radiant California tan solemnly intoned, "Though a spokesman for the City Attorney's office indicated that the atrocity will be judged self-defense, the self-righteous butchery of the fascist vigilante Lou Stevens will not go unpunished.

"Today, the Los Angeles Youth Action Corporation, a volunteer nonprofit corporation dedicated to the service of the Greater Los Angeles community, announced they will provide unlimited legal services to the families of the executed and mutilated teenagers to prosecute a civil action against the madman. A LAYAC attorney served the madman with papers initiating a five-hundred-million-dollar wrongful-death lawsuit in the death-squad-style execution of the five young men.

"The Los Angeles Youth Action Corporation has a long history of social activism. Time and time again, the chairman of the corporation, Mario Silva, and his staff of volunteers, have proved what brothers and sisters in struggle can accomplish if they put their ideals into action. K-Marx salutes LAYAC on yet another demonstration of concern and commitment."

The screen flashed the station-identification logo, a red, white and blue upraised fist superimposed over a red star, then the station's UHF channel number. Mark Lannon reappeared on screen.

A bruise blackened one eye. A patch of white adhesive tape covered his nose. More tape covered the side of his face. He did not speak for a moment to allow his audience to view his injuries, then finally announced in his shrill nasal whine, "Los Angeles Police officers inflicted these injuries. In a brutal and unprovoked attack on myself and two of this station's news personnel, the plainclothes storm troopers beat us and smashed our equipment. Though we lost the videotape of the scene, they did not stop the truth. Though the forces of reaction and blue-suit fascism may inflict casualties, they cannot stop the truth. The truth shall prevail.

"As we revealed in our earlier broadcast, one of the police officers involved in the suburban butchery perpetrated by Lou Stevens went berserk with blood lust and attacked his partners. We went to the Medical Center Intensive Care Ward where the Los Angeles Police Department holds the psychopathic killer-cop incommunicado.

"I intended to announce a major break in the case against the police-state regime striking out against the people of Los Angeles. I intended to make the announcement with the closed door and the shoulder-to-shoulder guards as a symbol of the oppressive regime threatening our freedoms.

"As we began taping the phalanx of officers guarding the entry, one of the plainclothes pigs turned off the lights. In the nightmare that followed, I and my two technicians suffered numerous injuries. The pigs destroyed our equipment. After they fled the room, we heard laughter and jokes as they celebrated their victory over three newspeople of this city.

"We lost the symbolic image. But that is nothing.

"I will reveal the breakthrough now. I predict the national implication will shake the present cowboy administration from power.

"In the years following the defeat of United States imperialism and its fascist running-dog lackeys in Vietnam, the quote leaders unquote of our oppressed nation have repeatedly told the people of our country of the billions of dollars in weapons and munitions lost to the victorious liberators of South Vietnam. Generals and colonels and counterterrorist specialists have warned of the eventual use of the weapons against the world.

"Throughout the past two years, White House spokesmen have announced the capture in Central America of weapons supposedly bearing serial numbers indicating they came from stockpiles captured in Vietnam.

"We now know this to be a total fabrication.

"Information furnished to me by a person of conscience inside the federal government reveals an automatic weapon was found at the scene of the slaughter at the home of Lou Stevens. This weapon, with the military identification code of XM-177, later known as Colt Automatic Rifle or Colt Commando Rifle, bore no serial number. The serial number had been ground away."

Mario Silva dropped his bourbon. Wide-eyed, he stared at the screen as Mark Lannon continued his report.

"However, the advanced technology of the Federal Bureau of Investigation raised a latent image of the defaced number from the metal of the weapon.

"Defense Department records indicate the People's Army of Vietnam captured this weapon during the liberation of the South. But how did this weapon appear in the segregated suburb where Lou Stevens makes his home?

"Because this weapon had not been captured by

the Vietnamese! Because this weapon has been warehoused for years in the armories of the United States! Because the fascist leadership of the United States had perpetrated a fraud upon the people of this country and the world!

"These weapons have appeared in Central America. Now we know who distributed the weapons! Not the People's Liberation Forces, but the Central Intelligence Agency!

"Now these weapons have appeared in Los Angeles! What fraud will the fascists now present to the gullible bourgeoisie? Communist conspiracy? International terrorism? Vietnamese infiltration?

"We know the truth. This is Mark Lannon, a man of the people speaking from K-Marx, the alternative to the fascist media, the voice of truth, wishing you good night and warning you.

"Lock your doors and shutter your windows. Arm yourselves. Stand ready. The fascist assault on our freedoms has already begun. Power to the people. Let the truth be known!"

As K-Marx switched to the weather report, Mario Silva went to his telephone. "Raphael? It's Mario. We have a problem with a shipment. I think one of our people released an article without authorization. Get your men and a truck. We need to check the inventory and ask some questions."

As he talked on the phone, the young playboy lawyer took a Beretta 92-S automatic from his office drawer. He slipped the pistol into his waistband at the small of his back.

Then he took out a folding straight razor. He flicked out the gleaming blade. "What if? No ifs! He will answer. He will tell us everything!"

The capture of the weapon linked LAYAC to a terrorist operation unknown even to Mario Silva's Cuban masters.

7

Fernando Ruiz put the silver tube to the black mirror of polished onyx.

A line of pure crystalline cocaine, finely chopped and sifted, sparkled on the onyx like a mountain of diamonds rising from a black ocean.

With a finger pressing his left nostril closed, he snorted half the line up his right nostril. Then he switched sides and put the other half up his left nostril.

Falling back on the leather-upholstered couch, Ruiz closed his eyes to the exhilaration racing through his nervous system. His body seemed to float and vibrate in space; his mind pulsed purple behind the stars of his eyes, his arms and legs became flashes of radiating light, his beating heart the spinning orb of a protogalaxy.

All the flesh and organs of his body seemed space-splendorous with cocaine, every cell a star in the infinite black of space.

Except for his nose, which was a black hole of darkness and absence of pleasure, the membranes numb from days of intense cocaine snorting.

But no blood yet, he thought, the image real yet

distant, fear merely an abstract thought in his or-
bit of pleasure. The crystalline coke hadn't cut his
membranes up that much. I'll snort till I bleed,
then maybe. . . .

Freebase. He'd never before had enough cocaine at one time to reverse the refining process
and precipitate coca paste for smoking.

Oh, yeah, freebase. When I'm bleeding, I'll
drop some 'ludes and crash for a day or so. Then
I'll get myself a freebasing kit. Do this right. Go
totally through the top. Hyperspace!

In the silence of the condominium, he heard the
click of his telephone-answering machine as it in-
tercepted another call. Set to take the call and
message without ringing, the machine kept his co-
workers at LAYAC away. Even if they came to his
complex, they had to call his phone number to
buzz his condo. And then the machine would intercept the call. Without an electronic key-signal
from the owner or occupant of the unit, the visi-
tors could not enter.

Let them bust through the iron fences and test
the guards. Oh, yeah. Boom-boom. That's the ad-
vantage of a security complex. Keep my riffraff
friends at a distance.

While I go through a kilo of cocaine.
Ohhhhhh. . . .

Even as he thought of the plastic bag in his
freezer, he did not believe it actually existed. He
had traded the machine gun for it, he had tested
the cocaine again, he had spooned out a handful,

he had resealed it and put in the freezer, but he could not believe it was real.

A kilo.

Could he snort it all? Could he freebase it and smoke it? Would he need to buy some hypos and needles? Could he buy intravenous equipment and drip it into a vein? No. . . .

He'd die.

Too much. If he divided the kilo in halves, kept one pound and sold the other pound, he'd get. . . .

Working the mathematics, he came up with $32,000.

He could put a down payment on a condo of his own—instead of this LAYAC unit.

Or a Porsche? A Mercedes? Lamborghini?

What did he want?

His laughter answered. Cocaine. That's all.

"You watch the news, Fernando?"

The voice shocked him upright. Hands seized his shoulders, another hand pressed down on his mouth to silence him.

Mario Silva, the chairman of LAYAC, stood in the center of the living room. He jangled a set of keys.

As the chairman of LAYAC, Silva had the key to the security condominium complex.

Three "street workers," wide-shouldered hard-faced ex-cons supposedly hired to mediate gang disputes but who actually served as Silva's enforcers, gripped Fernando Ruiz, holding him silent and immobile on the couch.

"Did you see the news tonight, Fernando?" Silva repeated. He glanced to his hired ex-cons. "Let him answer. You make any noise, we'll cut your balls off right now, right here. Now answer me."

To emphasize his questions, Silva opened a straight razor.

His eyes going wide, Ruiz stared at the gleaming blade. "No, I—"

"Then let me tell you what I heard on the news tonight." With the toe of his handmade shoe, Silva swept aside the ivory cigarette lighter and cut-crystal flower vase. He sat on the onyx table directly in front of Ruiz, his knees touching the youth counselor's knees.

"What I heard on the news was that the police have an XM-177. You know, one of those little M-16s. Now why do the police have one of those?"

"How could the pigs have that?" Fernando asked, not comprehending.

"That's what I'm asking you. Last night, some of the brothers went crazy on the petty bourgeoisie. And one gang got wiped out. And what did the cops come up with? An XM-177. What I want to know is this: is it one of ours?"

Ruiz had dreamed up the answer when he traded the black punk for the rifle. Now, the story did not sound right. But he had no other story.

"Yeah. Right. He said Shabaka sent him over for a weapon. That they needed one and some ammo. That was what I was supposed to do, right?"

"Did I give you the order?"

"No—"

"Then why did you—"

"Shabaka told—"

"He didn't tell you anything. How many rifles did you give the gangs?"

"Only one. The brother who Shabaka sent over—I gave him—"

"Don't lie to me!"

"Only one. I thought—"

"You thought wrong."

Silva signaled to his "street workers."

The three hoods jerked him from the leather couch and marched him across the condo, one hood gripping each arm, one behind him. Ruiz felt steel press into his back.

A hood told him, "You're going with us. Make any noise and we kill you, you know? You gonna make any problems?"

"No. Not me. I'm cool."

The hoods laughed. Ruiz saw Silva smile at the remark and the laughter.

Fernando Ruiz knew they would kill him.

They don't want to do it here, he realized. They'll take me someplace. Someplace where they can kill me and dump me. But they're trying to make me think they won't. Dig it, you got to make them think you believe them!

"Shabaka sent them. Why don't you ask him?"

"We'll talk about that with him," Silva told him. "Now you're cooperating. You don't cooperate, we shoot you down, understand me?"

"Anything you want to know...."

Silva swung open the door. In the last minutes of the smoggy Hollywood afternoon, the sky gray, the air gray, the pool and landscaping of the complex grayed by the smoggy air, the five men left the condo. The three ex-con "street workers" stayed close, hands gripping his arms to restrain Ruiz. They went down the stairs to the underground garage.

The hoods released their grip on Ruiz as they descended. Silva and a hood walked ahead of him. The other two stomped down the stairs behind him. At the bottom of the stairwell, the first hood shoved open the fire door to the garage and held it open for the group.

Five steps in front of him, Ruiz saw a convertible waiting. The blond young man behind the wheel revved the engine impatiently as he waited to exit the underground structure. He eased forward, the Fiat's front bumper almost touching the steel security gate as it rolled aside.

Ruiz shoved past Silva and dived. As the hoods shouted, Ruiz opened the door and landed by the driver in the front seat. His legs screaming with pain where they hit the top of the convertible's door, his head jammed between the bucket seats, he reached down and pushed the gas pedal with his hand.

In the confusion and shouting, the driver popped the clutch. Tires squealing, the Fiat lurched up the ramp to the street.

"They want to kill me! Get me out of here. Get away from—"

The driver whipped through a screeching right turn. He slowed as he grabbed Ruiz.

"Get out of my car, you crazy!" the driver shouted into the cocaine freak's face.

When a bullet shattered the windshield, the driver screamed and swerved and floored the accelerator.

Fernando Ruiz had less than a minute of freedom. Then a black-and-white squad car stopped the careering sports car.

8

In a tobacco-stinking lounge of Los Angeles International Airport, Carl Lyons and Flor Trujillo watched a jet taxi to a passenger-loading bridge. To bring it the last hundred feet to the bridge, field technicians had coupled a tug's tow-bar to the jet's front landing-gear strut. The tug docked the jet.

For a moment, Lyons took his attention from the runway. His eyes focused on the plate glass in front of them, on the mirrored image of himself and Flor standing together, his arm over her shoulders, like lovers waiting for arriving friends.

Flor had been quiet in the hours since the horror of the morgue. Though her professional demeanor tended toward silence broken by incisive observations—in contrast to Lyons's thoughtless comments and brutal joking—neither of them approached their time together as "on-duty time." In contrast to Flor the professional, Flor the lover joked and teased and gossiped. Carl Lyons had always considered the time he enjoyed with Flor to be precious.

The past times together—in the Caribbean or Washington, D.C., or New York—in the few hours or days their schedules allowed them to be together, he escaped from the discipline of the hard-core fighter. Flor knew his work. She also understood his reflexes.

Once, at breakfast in New York, with early morning traffic racing past a small café, an incoming customer opened the front door exactly as a truck backfired three times, one-two-three, like the firing of a large-caliber autopistol or a battle rifle with a low cyclic rate.

Lyons, seated at a small chrome-and-vinyl café table, had jumped simultaneously up and to the side. However, the table, bolted to the floor, had stopped him. The impact of his legs and torso against the table had overturned the water and juice glasses. Their breakfast plates clattered across the vinyl tabletop. All the waitresses and other diners stared at the big tanned man.

But Flor, knowing why Lyons had jumped, laughed. After a second, even as his heart raced with adrenaline, Lyons laughed, too.

Flor understood his silences and sudden rages. She understood his strange jokes. She understood his extreme generosity.

Now Lyons studied the lovely young woman beside his image in the plate glass. In her high heels, she stood only half a head short of his own height. She wore a modest summer dress with an abstract motif. Yet on her, the modest dress revealed and celebrated her body; a belt at her waist accentuated her slender form, her full breasts; the pale blue fabric contrasted engagingly with her dark skin and ink-black hair.

He touched the smooth fabric of the dress while his eyes watched his hand stroke her shoulder. In the reflection, she turned to him. He watched her profile as she looked to his face. He studied her while she studied him.

Overcome with a sudden desire to hold her, to touch her, to taste her, he pulled her against him.

One arm around her shoulders, the other hand on the muscled arch of the small of her back, he held her, feeling her breath on his neck, the rise and fall of her breasts against his shirt as she breathed. He kissed her, lightly, only wanting the sensation of her lips against his, to smell the warmth and moisture of her breath.

Brushing his face over her hair—she wore no perfume, used a shampoo without scent—then putting his face against the side of her neck, he smelled her sweat. The sweet yet acrid scent of her summer-sweating flesh struck memories, which came like flames, memories of the previous night, of her sweat glistening on her body. . . .

His hands clawed her against him in the passenger lounge.

Flor laughed as she eased away. "We're in public, you animal."

He pulled her against him again and whispered,

"We'll go to another motel. Maybe a hotel. The Bonaventure. Soon as we drop them off."

"Think it makes a difference, a motel or a hotel?"

"Not to me. Someplace where we can laugh."

Lyons glanced past the waiting crowd.

No passengers came from the jet bridge. Then a technician opened the doors to the lounge. The first passengers came a second later.

Hand in hand, Lyons and Flor went to meet his partners. They passed returning vacationers, businessmen, elderly travelers, women with babies in their arms. Friends and families welcoming the passengers talked and laughed all around them. But many of the travelers had returned to Los Angeles reluctantly. Lyons heard snatches of conversation.

"Think we'll be safe on the way home?"

"Did you bring a gun for me?"

"The east-coast news people—they say it's a war zone."

"The newspaper made a joke of it. Crazy Californians on cocaine."

"Is it true they're cannibals?"

Then Flor saw the two ex-Green Berets in casual clothes. Gadgets Schwarz and Rosario Blancanales followed the flow of the departing passengers. Gripping Lyons's hand, she pulled him through the crowd.

Gadgets blinked when he saw Flor. "Long time no see, Señora Meza."

"Thought you were on business," Blancanales remarked, giving Lyons a wink. The Puerto Rican charmer put an arm around Flor. "Glad to see you again. But why do you have to hang around with him? It won't do your reputation any good."

"Cut the crap," Lyons told his partners. "Let's go. You brought luggage?"

"You expect us to wear the same clothes all week?" Gadgets said. "Or do you think we can do this overnight?"

Lyons shook his head. "I got other plans for tonight. We'll take you downtown, introduce you to the blue-suits—"

"Ix-nay, Ironman," Gadgets interrupted as the group went to the escalator leading down from the passenger lounges. "Even if they're your friends, we got to stay far, far away."

"More congressmen call the Man?" Lyons asked.

Lyons rode shoulder-to-shoulder with Flor, Gadgets one step ahead, Blancanales one step back. They effectively blocked out any possibility of the nearby people overhearing them as they talked.

"You mean Hal, or the Main Man?" Gadgets said, turning to ride backward on the escalator.

"Any congressmen calling anybody."

"Just standard paranoia. Nothing special going on back east."

Blancanales leaned forward and spoke quietly. "But elections are coming up. One of our national voices of reason and social compassion would very much enjoy putting any one of us in Leavenworth. That would get him on the news three nights straight. So we need to stay invisible all the time.''

Gadgets stared at Blancanales for an instant, his eyes and mouth wide with mock shock. Then he grinned to Flor. ''The Pol never used to talk like that. Used to be soft words and brotherly understanding. It's hanging around with him—'' Gadgets pointed at Lyons ''—that's got our Rican talking this reactionary hard-core line.''

''Me?'' Lyons startled, actually offended. ''Me, reactionary?''

Gadgets put up his hands, whispered, ''I'm your friend, don't kill me. Don't kill me. Remember, you'd have to carry fifty percent more equipment.''

''*Calmatese, mi hermano,*'' Blancanales laughed, his hands on Lyons's shoulders. ''Perhaps he meant it as a compliment.''

''I'm calm, just quit the clowning.''

They left the escalator. Walking in a tight group through the underground corridor from the passenger lounges and the terminal, the four counterterrorists hurried past slower travelers.

''Your luggage heavy?'' Lyons asked his partners.

Gadgets nodded. ''Very heavy. Someone steal our suitcases, they could start a war.''

''Don't even say it,'' Lyons commented.

"L.A.'s got one army of crazies out there already. An army of doper zombies."

They continued to the crowded baggage pickup area. Knowing the traps and frustrations of international airports, Lyons waited until Gadgets and Blancanales took their bags from the oval conveyor belt before he and Flor went for their parked rental car.

Minutes later they sped from the international airport. Lyons navigated the car through the stream of traffic on Century Boulevard. They passed high-rise hotels and rows of pornographic bookstores and "adult cinemas." Gadgets peered out at the neon and lurid billboards.

"This specialist work we do is so amazing," he said. "One day in Bolivia, the next in California. I never get tired of this, the places we go, the things we do."

Flor turned to the men in the back seat and said, "Do you think we can make any difference? Only the four of us?"

Blancanales laughed. "Miss Trujillo, if you only knew...."

"We make things different," Gadgets nodded. "Wherever we go. Good or bad, things get changed. In fact, dig it, Ironman—Konzaki's taking a seminar in robotics. Says he's going to replace us. With titanium Godzillas."

Flor waited for the laughter to stop, then pressed her question. "But there are many police—thousands—already working. How can only four more make any difference?''

''We'll see what we can do and do it,'' Gadgets responded.

''That's it,'' Lyons agreed. ''That is it.''

On the freeway, Blancanales and Gadgets noticed the empty lanes. On most weekday evenings, drivers commuting home late from work or early for the theaters and nightspots of the metropolis would crowd the freeways. Not tonight.

''Where is everybody?'' Gadgets asked. ''Usually, there's more traffic than this after one in the morning.''

''The murders?'' Blancanales asked.

''What do you think?'' Lyons asked him. ''After a day and night of continuous media hype and on-the-spot video gore....''

''Fear City,'' Gadgets commented.

Half an hour of driving took them to the Civic Center. Lyons drove down into the guarded and patrolled underground garage for city employees. Their ''federal'' identification persuaded a uniformed officer to issue a guest sticker.

At the reception desk of Parker Center, Lyons again flashed his federal identification. ''We're here to talk to Detective Towers.''

''Took you long enough to get here,'' the desk cop answered. ''Detective Towers told me to expect you. Interrogation's been going on for two hours.''

''Interrogation of who?''

"Not anything I know about. But they got him the room with the mirrors."

As soon as the desk officer issued four identification badges, the group rushed for the third floor. Uniformed and plainclothes officers crowding the corridor glared at the strangers.

"Who are you?" a sergeant demanded.

"Towers invited us to listen in," Lyons told him.

"Oh, yeah?" The sergeant turned to another officer. "Check with Bill."

"Who have they got in there?"

"That's for Detective Towers to say."

"Hey, Sergeant," Lyons protested, offended by the interdepartmental hostility. "We're on your side."

"Yeah, they all say that."

Bill Towers rushed from the interrogation room. He opened another door and motioned the four Federals inside. He waited until the door closed to tell them, "We got our break."

"One of the punks?" Lyons asked.

Grinning, Towers shook his head. "Not a punk. A superpunk. We got the one who gave them the rifle. He recruited the punks, his organization trained them, and he gave them the rifle."

The four Federal specialists glanced to one another.

Bill Towers continued, his voice rising with enthusiasm. "We got a chance. We got a chance to break them. Tonight!"

9

Shabaka, a mullah of Allah and a warrior in the Holy War against the white devils of Satan, received the command to disperse his soldiers and dismantle or destroy his indoctrination center.

At seven o'clock, Mario Silva, the chairman of LAYAC, telephoned Shabaka with the information of the capture of Ruiz. Silva told him that Ruiz would undoubtedly betray the organization to the police to save himself from prison. Shabaka had answered in monosyllables, then hung up the telephone.

Abdul Shabaka, born with the devil name of Leroi Jackson, had known from the first day that the betrayal of the bourgeois front organization would be only a matter of time.

As a veteran of the Black Panthers, the Death's Angels and the Black Liberation Army, he knew any organization risked infiltration and betrayal. The FBI had infiltrated and neutralized the Panthers. Informers had betrayed the holy Muslim warriors of the Death's Angels to the San Francisco police. Informers had broken the Black Liberation Army.

Even as a teenage recruit in the Black Panthers, Shabaka recognized the inevitable defeat of any open organization. The Panther leadership had welcomed him, a rapist and petty thief, because of his juvenile record of crimes against whites. They knew little else of his life. He had expected a careful check into his past and a long interrogation. But the Panthers had accepted him after listening to his stories of "revolutionary acts against the slavemakers." This easy entry to the revolutionary organization surprised him. As the numbers of Panthers grew, each new recruit joining with the same ease, he knew the organization had swallowed the seeds of its own destruction.

The Panthers made no secret of their goals. The leaders published manifestos of racial hatred. At rallies, they pranced and posed in their leather jackets and preached social justice through the murder of police officers. They spat out their black racist diatribes from stages or in front of the microphones of radical radio stations.

The Panthers knew all about the police surveillance. Police followed the Panthers everywhere, recording their words, photographing each leader and his aides and their friends. The ex-con leaders of the Panthers gloried in the surveillance. They accepted surveillance as an affirmation of the Black Panther Party as a threat to white racist society and the fascist corporate power structure.

At meetings and rallies, the teenage Leroi Jackson looked at the young militants around him and wondered who worked for the police and who worked for the FBI. Other Panthers—the hard-core felons who'd had experience with prison informers—also believed the police slipped agents into the organization. The hard-core Panthers developed techniques to discover the agents; they initiated surveillance of one another, they investigated backgrounds, and they launched "actions."

The Panther leadership had often talked of "strikes against the fascist monster." The hard-core Panthers screened the membership and identified the recruits they doubted. Then they invited these recruits on actions: the assassination of a detective, the driveby strafing of a police station, the bombing of a city councilman's office.

At first, the police acted immediately on their agents' information and struck the Panthers. But they found the hard-core killers waiting quietly in their apartments, without explosives, without illegal weapons, without any weapons whatsoever.

Antiterrorist detectives cautioned their remaining agents and informers to wait until the Panthers actually put a conspiracy in motion. But the Panthers varied their techniques; sometimes they organized an attack, then as the "front line brothers" approached the target, they canceled the hit, replanned and announced another time. This forced the agents to contact their officers again and again. That was how the Panthers caught them. Some agents died. Others fled.

Leroi Jackson fled the Panthers for the closed society of the Nation of Islam. He joined a radical sect obsessed with hatred and racism, where he found many other young blacks who shared his lust for violence against whites. In obedience to the leaders who preached myths of pale, blue-eyed creatures bred by the Devil to plague the world, a group of felons and psychopaths created a secret cult of random racial murder.

The Death's Angels believed they followed the will of their prophet. In San Francisco, Los Angeles, Oakland and in the cities of the East, gangs of fervent Black Muslims roamed the streets and highways to murder whites.

White hitchhikers, white pedestrians, white shoppers died when shotguns fired from passing cars. Others died as unknown blacks attacked with machetes.

The Nation of Islam never accepted responsibility for the horror inspired by their hatred. Meanwhile the Death's Angels continued untouched in their random terror, and they gained courage. They abandoned quick murder by bullets or machetes for the more satisfying ritual of murder by mutilation.

Kidnapping whites, groups of Angels used pliers and soldering irons and saws to reduce "white devils" to screaming masses of tortured meat; eyes gone, hands gone, their limbs scorched and broken, white devils became sacrifices to a cruel medieval god worshiped by the welfare-state spawn of the long-past Arab and European slave trade.

In accordance with Muslim doctrine, Leroi Jackson had become Abdul Shabaka. And in obedience to Death's Angels racial hatred, he became a murderer of whites. He shotgunned a young girl hitchhiking beside a freeway ramp. He joined in the rape and mutilation-murder of a San Francisco woman, keeping one of her fingers as proof of his service to the Prophet.

Shabaka also aided in the indoctrination of other hateful young blacks who lacked the psychopathic intensity required to fight in the war of extermination against the white devils.

Shabaka assembled thousands of photographs, thousands of feet of film of white cruelty to blacks. In a time when the white middle-class hippies took drugs and stared for hours at the abstract pulsating colors of psychedelic light shows, Shabaka presented Death's Angels initiates with multimedia assaults of images and voices of white racism and white hatred and white violence against blacks. He flashed a thousand images of blacks horribly mutilated and murdered by the KKK, the American Nazi Party and racist police throughout colonial and American history. He also taught the initiates to hate nonrevolutionary blacks—the "Uncle Toms," the Americans of African ancestry who sought their share of opportunity and prosperity as the United States ended the centuries of law-sanctioned oppression of their race. The teenage black punks, twisted by lives of poverty and suffering in the well-intentioned welfare state, twisted again by the circulated agit-prop of the Black Muslims and the Death's Angels, became the roving shock troops of race war by random terror.

The San Francisco police succeeded in breaking one gang of Death's Angels. With the closing of the Zebra case, they solved fourteen murders of whites. But the police never brought to justice the other gangs murdering whites in other parts of California. Investigators never resolved the scores of other murders in California.

Shabaka took no comfort in that failure of law enforcement. Fearing informers, he fled to Algeria to join the surviving Black Panthers in exile.

There, he avoided the other North American black expatriates—or as they came to call themselves, the New Afrikan Freedom Fighters. He learned Arabic, the language of the slavers who had decimated the nations of Africa to supply slaves to Arabia and the European colonies, and Russian, the language of history's most powerful slave state.

The Soviet KGB had already bought control of the Palestinian and Pan-Arabic movements. Shabaka saw the Soviet weapons and munitions supplied to the Arabs and knew where to seek support in his continuing war against North American whites. Though white themselves, Soviets listened to Shabaka's racist diatribes against whites and nodded their approval.

They saw him as a weapon to throw against the world's most successful revolution. With a thousand terror-warriors like Shabaka, the Soviets could rape the hope of an egalitarian United States. With the horror of a black-extremist race war racking Americans, counterterror and counteratrocity—whites against blacks, whites against Meso and South Americans, whites against any non-European foreigners—became certainties. And every incident of white backlash would be featured in the KGB's worldwide media machine as horrors, thus winning a propaganda victory for the Soviet monsters who armed and dispatched the terrorists.

As he had no outstanding indictments, Shabaka risked traveling between the United States and Algeria. He arranged for the smuggling of weapons and money to the Black Liberation Army, a gang of heroin and cocaine addicts seeking revenge for their years in prison through the assassinations of police and federal officers.

It was Shabaka, in the early years of the eighties, who found Mario Silva, the son of Batista fascists, who had sold himself to the new general who ruled Cuba. For a million dollars a year, Silva provided Shabaka with the pick of the black and Chicano teenage offenders in LAYAC's youth programs. He told Silva that he trained the young men and women for the "Revolution." Shabaka kept his operation separate from all other LAYAC concerns. He pretended to be only an aging revolutionary black lawyer who took time off from his legal practice to help juvenile delinquents.

But Silva had learned of the weapon shipments. He claimed a few of the automatic rifles and grenades for his own enforcers and allowed Shabaka to keep all the others. They maintained a good working relationship.

When Shabaka learned of Silva's involvement in the KGB plot to depopulate Los Angeles with binary nerve gas, he began to admire the Cuban to a certain extent. But he never told Silva about his new deal, never mentioned the sponsors who were now backing him to establish a terror center in the United States. Unlimited funds from the Soviets and Libya had produced a drug never before known to the drug subculture. The extremely addicting drug had the effect of instantly creating a psychopath who felt no pain or remorse or human limitations, who would strike at any nearby target. His qualifications had earned Shabaka the privilege of launching an army of devil zombies to attack North American whites.

Shabaka's killers remained secret, insulated from all possible betrayal.

Then came the phone call. Against Silva's orders, without Shabaka's knowledge, one of Silva's lieutenants had given an automatic rifle to a gang of punks. The capture of the rifle meant that a law-enforcement task force would investigate the entire LAYAC structure.

As the end of Shabaka's operation neared, he had no regrets. He had trained a hundred black and Chicano punks. He had indoctrinated them in the hatred and murder of whites. Though he now could not train the thousand he wanted, the experiment had succeeded. He had sent out the three kill-squads to test the combination of drugs and indoctrination. The test had been a complete success.

Now, he would release all one hundred of the chemically enraged zombie warriors. As the terror seized Los Angeles, he would escape.

10

Neon gave life to a night without laughter or joy. Lyons cruised through East Los Angeles, surveying the dark, silent residential streets, the shops on the deserted boulevards.

Families did not brave the streets. No one sat at the tables of restaurants and cafés. A theater had turned off its marquee lights. Supermarkets had closed their doors.

Few cars moved on the streets, only cruising gang cars and infrequent police black-and-whites on patrol.

Groups of Chicano punks loitered on street corners. Latin disco rhythms and loud voices came from oversized portable stereos. Others stood near the open doors of their cars, their auto stereos blasting. The groups stared at the passing Ford, eyes on every street squinting to look inside the dark interior of the car.

As they approached the LAYAC address, Lyons knew that any one of the hundred gang punks could be a loco with a concealed walkie-talkie or a dime for a pay phone. Gang boys could be watching from the rooftops of the apartments.

Flor rode beside Lyons. In the back seat of the rented car, Towers worked a cassette player. The voices from the Parker Center interrogation room filled the interior of the car.

"The blacks and vatos are soldiers, right, for enforcing dope deals? So when they wanted the rifle, I traded it—"

"You mean the Colt Automatic Rifle," a police interrogator interrupted.

"Yeah. The little machine gun. They gave me a kilo of coke for it."

"A kilo? What're you talking about?"

"Yeah. A kilo. They ripped it off some rich lawyer in Beverly Hills."

"The punks didn't want it?"

"Nah, man, they said it was nothing—"

Towers punched the stop button. "You hear that? The punks didn't want the cocaine. Listen to this...."

The recorded voice of Ruiz continued. *"They were high on something else."*

"What? Heroin?"

"They didn't act stoned. They acted insane."

"That's one interesting part," Towers told them, clicking off the player again. "After he traded the rifle for the cocaine, he arranged a phony burglary of the warehouse to suggest that the punks stole the rifle. But that was set for tonight. The FBI traced the rifle too quick. And then someone in the Bureau leaked it to that crazy Communist television station. And the boss of

LAYAC, this Silva guy, found out about it and went after our boy Ruiz.''

Lyons thought for a moment. He glanced in the rearview mirror to see the lights of the car that Blancanales drove. As Lyons eased through a slow left-hand turn on the deserted avenue, he asked Towers, "Why did Ruiz have the rifle in the first place?"

"He said there was a 'heat wave,' " Towers answered. "Right after that problem with the gas, remember? If you know what I mean?"

"Flor was in on that," Lyons told him. "You can talk about it."

"Good. Trying to keep all that classified info and authorization and clearance jazz straight makes my head spin. Right after your people wiped out that gang, the Feds put LAYAC under the microscope."

"Then why didn't they—"

"Because they didn't get the chance! The investigation had only got started, they put in a day or two of questioning, then the Feds get calls from every politician in the country. All of them concerned about LAYAC's good name. But in those two days of 'heat,' they had an arms shipment come in before the politicians pulled the plug on the investigation. Ruiz was the only one that didn't have Federals parked outside his door. He picked up the rifles and stored them until Silva and that Shabaka could divide up the boxes."

"Who brought in the weapons?" Lyons asked.

"Some Mexican trucking company. One of LAYAC's companies."

"Convenient."

"That's what LAYAC seems to be all about. But listen to this—"

The voices of the interrogators and Ruiz spoke again. *"What was that?"*

"The third phase."

"What does that mean?"

"I don't know. I wasn't supposed to hear that. A weird spade called Shabaka said it to one of his assistants. Said the rifles could stay in the warehouse until the third phase."

"But the third phase of what?" The interrogator pressed.

"The gee-had. That's the word he used. Gee-had. Whatever that means."

Lyons knew the word too well. "Jihad. The Holy War. Hashish and Commie lies weren't enough, so they came up with a superdope."

"There, that place." Towers pointed at an apartment house decorated with spray-painted gang script. A group of young men in identical khaki pants and sleeveless white T-shirts lounged on the steps. Other knots of gang punks stood on the sidewalks and leaned against cars. They drank from bottles wrapped in brown paper bags.

"Public drinking and intoxication," Lyons commented. He glanced back to his ex-partner. "What do you say we just take them away?"

"No, thanks. I want to spend my pension."

"Two against twenty. We got them outnumbered."

"You do it. I want to see if the Feds taught you any special survival skills. Like how to reincarnate."

Laughing, Lyons coasted past the punks. He made a right turn, then he keyed his hand-radio. "That's the place. I see an alley back here. Garages."

"A whole lot of mean-looking dudes out front," Gadgets answered. "I don't know about getting in and out quiet. You want to rethink this?"

"Yeah, they got M-16s and grenades in there," Lyons said. "What happens when a hundred doped-up punks with automatic rifles go berserk?"

"That informer said the M-zipteens are upstairs?" Gadgets asked.

"That's where that organization has all the offices. Upstairs."

Lyons continued to the next block and parked in the darkness under a tree. In the rearview mirror, he watched the second rental car cruise past the alley.

Blancanales spoke through the radio, "The roof. We'll go up one of those other apartments, drop down into the office."

"Second the motion," said Gadgets's voice. "I don't want any firefights with that crowd on the street. I didn't pack that much ammunition."

Lyons turned to Flor and Towers. "My partners and I are going in. Bill, you stand by in one car. Flor, you drive the other one. We have a problem—things'll happen fast."

"This is for information only, yes?" Flor asked.

"We find those weapons, we'll call for the police."

"No heroes? Tell me, no heroes."

"Not me," Lyons assured her.

Two minutes later, Flor guided her car through the wide commercial alley. Lights illuminated rear entries and garages and parked cars. On the higher floors, balconies jutted from the back walls of the apartments.

The car rolled to a stop near a dumpster head-high with trash and garbage. The three men of Able Team slipped out into the alley's shadows.

The car eased away. At the end of the alley, it disappeared into the night. Surrounded by the trash and rotting filth, Able Team scanned the alley for movement. They carried no assault weapons. Their sports coats concealed their radios and shoulder-holstered autopistols. Gadgets carried a few hand tools and electronic devices in an airline bag.

Without a word, Lyons led them through the alley's darkness. He pointed to a derelict car sitting on four flat tires, then to the steel ladders and platforms of a fire escape above the alley.

The apartments' fire escapes doubled as balconies. Flowerpots and planter boxes covered the landings. Blancanales and Gadgets nodded. Lyons stepped up and onto the top of the derelict car. He tested the ladder, then went up quickly, his neoprene-soled shoes silent on the rungs.

Glancing into the lighted interior of the second-floor apartment as he passed, he saw a family gathered around a color television. A news commentator pointed to a map of Los Angeles. Lyons continued. In the next apartment, two young girls—perhaps ten years old—danced to a North American rock-and-roll standard sung in Spanish.

Lyons stopped at the top of the fire-escape ladder. He eased his head up over the wall and scanned the rooftop. The black silhouettes of vent pipes and antennas stood against the distant lights of downtown's high-rise towers.

The diffuse gray light reflected from the polluted night sky revealed a tar roof littered with trash and beer cans. Lyons snaked over the top. Crouching in a shadow, he unhooked his hand-radio from his belt.

"You two. I'm on top. Waiting for you." Lyons looked around. "Flor. You monitoring?"

"Monitoring," she answered.

"Mr. Detective see anything out front?"

"Zero. Will tell you if."

The steel ladder vibrated with steps. In seconds, Blancanales swung over the wall, followed by Gadgets.

Motionless in the shadows, they listened. City

noises and snatches of music came from the streets below. A ventilator fan grated in its housing, ejecting the smells of cooking oils and mildewed apartments into the warm night air.

Moving again, Lyons crouch-walked toward the roof of the adjoining building. He felt his way past the guy wires of antennas, his eyes continuously sweeping the shadows and forms ahead of him for the motions of a sentry. He heard only the faint cracking of dust and grit under his shoes.

At the edge of the roof, he waited again as two shadows followed him. They peered over the low wall to the next building.

A loud stereo played beneath them. The tar of the roof, still warm from the summer sun, throbbed with the disco beat.

The bricks of the two apartment buildings met. There was no airspace or easement between the walls. Scanning the next roof, they saw another expanse of shadows and gray half darkness. They saw no motion on the next building or on the roof of the LAYAC building beyond.

"Electronic security?" Lyons hissed to Gadgets.

"You can hear it?"

"Hear what?"

"Listen...."

Straining their ears, Lyons and Blancanales listened. A motorcycle passed on the avenue, the staccato popping fading. Quiet returned. They heard a high-pitched whine. Then a low rider's loud muffler blasted the avenue.

"Ultra High Frequency motion sensor," Gadgets whispered as he searched through his bag of gear. "Plus they'll have pressure sensors. And someone standing guard. Look around for some pigeon shit."

"What are you talking about?"

"They have motion sensors. If pigeons fly around up here, they have false alarms—"

"Pigeons don't fly at night."

"Use your imagination. Find some bat shit."

A dog barked, once, twice, then went quiet.

The UHF whine cut off. They saw the silhouette of a man moving on the LAYAC roof.

"That makes it easy," Gadgets whispered.

Lyons tapped Blancanales and Gadgets. "Berettas... I'm going ahead. You follow."

Lyons crept over the roof to a fan housing. He stood up with the bulk of the housing behind him. He watched the far building, looking for movement. Then he hissed to the others.

He saw them approach, slinking through the antennas and vents. A tangle of razor wire, two coils high, stopped all three of them.

They spread out along the barrier of concertina razors. They knew the group inside the building would have provided for rooftop escape. The razor fence would have gates.

Blancanales went slowly, feeling ahead of him for security sensors or trash that might make noise. He peered up at the barbed wire, then moved along, fingers sweeping over the gritty tar. He found a bottle, then another; he set them far to the side.

Suddenly a shape directly in front of him blocked his view.

Hands seized him, pulled him into the tangle of steel razors.

11

Two blocks away, Flor Trujillo waited in the rented Ford, the engine idling, the front seat covered with radios.

A portable police-band radio scanned the department's communications, electronic noise and voices filling the interior of the car.

An encoded hand-radio provided for an instantaneous link to Able Team.

A second nonsecure walkie-talkie linked her to Detective Towers where he waited a few blocks to the west.

She watched the street around her. Nothing moved. Despite the warm night, no one sat on the porches or talked with neighbors. No children bicycled or played soccer in the brilliant blue white glare of the streetlights. When she parked, she had seen the curtains of the security-barred windows of several houses part as the residents peered out. But the people remained hidden in the safety of their homes.

From time to time, headlights streaked the boulevard. But no cars moved on the side street. Flor had set her rearview mirrors to provide overlapping views of the sidewalks and street behind her. As she waited for a signal from Able Team or Towers, she scanned her surroundings, her eyes always moving, from the neighborhood in front of her to the lawns and houses on the right and left, and to the images in the mirrors.

A chaos of voices erupted from the police-band scanner. Though Flor strained to understand, the police officers spoke in code words and numbers, only the urgency in their voices telling of what they faced. Then one voice said simply, "We're taking fire from the roof. Automatic-weapon fire! We're getting out of—"

A high-velocity shriek tore from the radio.

"They've got rockets! Someone up there's got—"

The band went blank for an instant, then other voices called out. Flor heard the word "ambush."

Turning down the radio's volume, she rolled down her window.

Autofire popped in the distance. She heard the tearing sound of a rocket and the crack of the explosion. Then came a sound only possible in that night of empty boulevards and unnatural quiet: the night screamed.

As police officers in a hundred squad cars all hit the same switch, sirens rose in one vast wail. The flooring of accelerators came next, by every officer—in uniform and plainclothes—who heard of the ambush.

Rolling up her window, Flor turned up the volume of the scanner. She heard a commander assigning response units. The commander ordered all other units to maintain their patrols. Flor keyed the Stony Man secure-circuit handradio.

"Able Team! This is Flor. Able Team!"

She waited for an answer. Then she keyed the transmit key again. "Able Team! Report. There has been—"

She heard autofire. This time not in the distance. The popping of automatic rifles came from the boulevard.

Slipping out her Detonics .45, she thumbed back the hammer to full cock. She slammed the rented Ford into gear and accelerated into the roar of the firefight.

SHOES SCUFFED on the asphalt roof. Lyons looked up to see Blancanales standing, his back arched, his hands gripping the hands closed around his throat. In the instant that Lyons evaluated the situation, two other forms appeared on the other side of the tangled concertina wire.

"*¡Hijo de puta!*" one voice spat out.

"*¿Quién es?*" another asked.

Then Lyons saw the silhouette of an AK-47 and heard the distinctive "clack" as a hand flicked the ComBloc weapon's safety to fire position.

In one smooth motion, Lyons swept out his reengineered and silenced Colt Government Model, his thumb flipping the fire selector down to three-shot burst. He put the dash-dot-dash of the tritium night sights on the silhouette showing the AK.

A burst of .45-caliber hollowpoints sprayed the form's lungs and heart into the night. Lyons put the sights on the next form, squeezed off another burst. The three instantaneous impacts threw the silhouette back.

A muzzle flashed, the report of an assault rifle blasted the quiet. Lyons aimed above the flash, triggered a burst, saw the form hurled back. He emptied the last cartridge from the extended ten-round magazine into the falling gunman.

Gasping for breath, Blancanales fell back from the concertina barrier. A dead man hung in the coils, hundreds of razor-points stuck in his arms holding him upright.

As Lyons dropped out the empty magazine and slapped in another, he heard Gadgets's Beretta zip slugs into a stairwell housing on the LAYAC roof. Nine-millimeter subsonic slugs hammered stucco, one slapped flesh. In the blackness of the doorway, someone gasped. A rifle clattered to the roof.

"In we go!" Lyons called out to his partners.

Gadgets answered. "Ironman, what the—"

"Now! Through the wire!"

Rushing to the concertina barrier, Lyons reached through the tangle of steel razors. He grabbed the hair of the dead man and jerked him against the wire. Lyons dragged the corpse toward him, forcing the wire down with the dead man's weight. The wire sagged. Pulling his arm clear, Lyons put his foot on the corpse and compressed the coils.

"Now!"

Lyons ran over the dead man's back. Reengineered Colt pointed at the stairway housing, Lyons snatched up an AK from the roof. He glanced at the sights. The ComBloc weapon had the clip-on night sights in place.

A muzzle flashed from the door. As slugs tore past his head, Lyons triggered a three-round burst. He did not slow in his rush. He saw movement and slammed it with the AK. As the form fell back, Lyons flicked his Colt's fire selector up to single shot. He killed the gunman as the guy raised a shadowy autorifle.

Gadgets checked Blancanales. His Puerto Rican partner pulled himself up.

"Cover me!" Blancanales scanned the roof ahead of him for movement, then scrambled over the corpse.

"This is crazy!" Gadgets said to no one. But he followed his partners.

At the head of the stairway, Lyons emptied the captured AK into the chest of a punk on the landing below. Dropping the empty magazine, he searched through the tangle of dead punks in the stairway housing. He found a loaded Kalashnikov and an Uzi. Blancanales grabbed a bloody AK and snapped shots down the stairs.

Gadgets ran up behind them. "Ironman, you gone crazy? I got two mags for my Beretta, and we're going into a firefight?"

"If they've got this many sentries—" Lyons passed the Uzi to Gadgets as the punks returned autofire "—they've got something important down below."

"Like an army," Blancanales answered.

"Something as important as us living through this?" Gadgets asked.

Flipping over a dead punk, Lyons found a web belt hung with AK mag pouches. "Two magazines, plus whatever's in the rifles. And this—" He held up one of two grenades he found in a pouch.

Blancanales searched other corpses and came across a belt pouch with two Uzi mags. He passed the pouch to Gadgets. A burst of AK fire roared past him and feet hammered on the stairs.

A wide-eyed, screaming punk sprinted up the stairs, his Kalashnikov flashing. Lyons stepped back, waited an instant, then fired two rounds from his own Kalashnikov point-blank into the screaming punk's chest.

Flesh and fragments of bone exploded from his back as the punk slammed sideways into the stucco of the stairwell housing. He did not fall.

Staring around him, the punk saw Lyons and Blancanales. Screaming as he staggered forward, his face twisted with hatred, blood spraying from the two lung wounds, he swung his AK toward Blancanales.

Lyons put the muzzle of his captured Ka- lashnikov under the chin of the punk and fired. Impact lifted the bleeding, mortally wounded teenager off his feet, the blast tear- ing away the side of his head. But still he did not fall.

Screaming, his shattered jaw yawning, blood frothing from his mangled throat, the punk lurched forward again. Lyons grabbed the barrel of the punk's AK and jerked him off balance.

The punk staggered from the stairwell. Gadgets stepped up behind the punk and put his captured Uzi at the base of the punk's skull. A burst severed the brain from the spinal cord.

"Take his weapon," Lyons told Gadgets.

"This is insane! I'm not going down there! There could be a hundred of them!"

Lyons jerked the cotter pin from the first grenade. A storm of autofire came from below, then more feet hammered the stairs. Berserk punks screamed with chemical rage. Lyons let the safety lever flip away, counted to four, then gave the grenade an underhand toss.

Standing to the side of the roof door, he raised his AK. The first punk out the door took a through-and-through head wound from a Com- Bloc slug. Still screaming, he fell and kicked as his life spurted from his shattered skull.

A second punk ran from the stairwell as the grenade exploded below. Though the stairs and landing shielded the punk's body, steel fragments punched through the back of his head.

As if he did not feel the wounds, the punk continued advancing, streams of blood fountaining from his skull. Blancanales aimed at the punk's back and put a careful burst through the wounded punk's heart. Still screaming, with a vast wound where his heart had been, the punk continued on to the end of the roof. He hurtled into space.

From the stairwell they heard a bestial, inhuman sound. A sound like a dog's growl, but broken with gasps and choking. They saw a hand clutching a Kalashnikov, then the third punk crawled from the stairwell.

A hundred grenade fragments had shattered and ripped both legs. Dangling by only ligaments and a few strands of flesh, the legs flopped and twisted behind the punk. But obviously he did not feel the horrible wounds.

Clawing at the asphalt of the roof, he looked around for the attackers. Blancanales dispatched him to darkness with a burst to the back of his head.

The autofire from below slacked off. Absolutely astounded by what he had seen, Gadgets stared down at the finally dead teenager. Then the ex-Green Beret turned to Lyons.

"I'm not going down there. I don't care what

the fuck you say, Lyons. Call down an airstrike, call for tanks, call for the Marines, but I'm not going down there!''

Blancanales changed mags on his captured AK. "Second the motion. Motion carried. We retreat. Period. Follow me.''

"All right, all right,'' Lyons finally agreed. He took his hand-radio from his belt. "I need my Atchisson, anyway. Flor,'' he said into his hand-radio, "we got some heavy action here. We need our weapons.''

In the alley behind the apartments, skidding tires answered his call.

"Now that's a quick response,'' Gadgets commented.

"Go!'' Lyons shouted to his partners. "I'll cover.''

Gadgets and Blancanales, both holding captured autoweapons, dashed to the corpse spanning the wire. They jumped through the gap, then took positions to cover Lyons.

Sporadic autofire came from the stairwell. Lyons held his fire. He stuck a finger through the ring of the second grenade, then stopped.

He reached into the stairwell housing and grabbed one of the dead punks. He jerked the corpse out of the doorway, then slammed the door closed. He pushed the corpse against the door to hold it closed.

He devised a booby trap. He jerked the pin from the grenade and put the grenade between the corpse holding the door closed and the door itself. When the punks shoved the door open, the grenade would explode, maiming or killing the nearest pursuers, perhaps killing a few on the stairs.

Lyons grinned sardonically at a thought. Can't chase if they got no legs.

"Ironman!" Gadgets called out. "Move it! Flor says there's action in the alley."

The boom of a .45 spurred Lyons. A loaded AK in each hand, he ran for the corpse-bridge through the razor wire. The .45 boomed twice again. Autofire from an M-16 answered. A final shot from Flor's Detonics .45 silenced the Colt rifle.

Hurtling the gap, steel razors slashing one leg, Lyons passed Blancanales and Gadgets. He ran to the edge of the roof and looked down.

The rented Ford spun rubber, fishtailing through the alley. The car lurched as it thumped over a corpse, then raced away. Autofire—this time from a Kalashnikov—popped from the doorways beneath Lyons. The glass of the Ford's rear windshield shattered.

Skidding around the corner, the Ford disappeared from his sight. He jerked his hand-radio from his belt. Gadgets's shout stopped him.

"She's around the corner. Waiting for us So let's move it!"

The grenade booby trap exploded. Lyons followed Gadgets and Blancanales over the roofs.

Hearing the screams of the berserk punks, Lyons looked back. He saw a horror.

A punk pursued them. Lurching from side to side, moving oddly, the punk seemed to be only four feet tall. Then Lyons realized what he saw. The punk had lost both legs at the knees. Yet he did not fall. The punk continued forward, running on the stumps of his legs, an autorifle gripped in his hands.

Lyons carefully lined up the Kalashnikov's night-sight dots on the maimed, drug-enraged monster and shot the top of its head away.

Others came. Shrieking and screaming, they tried to thrash through the razor wire. The steel points slashed them but they did not notice. One of the punks found the gap and called out to the others.

Lyons fired again. He saw the guy's head explode. Then Lyons sprinted after his partners.

Gadgets covered the roof with his Uzi as Blancanales went down the fire escape. Lyons looked at the 9mm submachine gun in Gadgets's hands and shook his head.

"Forget that little popgun. Just go. I'll do what I can."

With a quick salute, Gadgets followed Blancanales. Lyons turned to the advancing gang. He took cover behind a fan housing. Easing the Kalashnikov's fire-selector lever to semiautomatic, he lined up the AK's glowing dots on the screaming mouth of a punk. The 7.62mm ComBloc slug punched through the mouth to explode the brain-stem. The punk dropped instantly.

Lyons methodically executed the next three punks. The drug gave them superhuman strength and rage but made them stupid. They did not take cover or advance in fire-teams. They only rushed at Lyons. And he killed them.

Snapping the magazine out of his second captured AK—the autorifle had no night sights—he shoved the magazine in his coat pocket. He slung the AK with night sights over his shoulder and ran to the ladder.

Without any attempt at silence, Lyons descended. He called out to his partners. "On my way down!"

A truck engine revved. Gears shifted. Lyons looked down as a five-ton truck marked LAYAC Farm Fresh Produce came from a garage. The truck gained speed. An autorifle extended from the passenger-side window, spraying fire wildly at the alley's shadows. Blancanales and Gadgets returned fire.

The truck swerved and bumped onto the side street where Flor waited. Lyons heard more auto-fire. Then the sound of the truck's engine faded.

Continuing to the alley, Lyons ran to where Flor waited. With Blancanales and Gadgets only a few steps behind him, Lyons jerked open the Ford's passenger front door.

"That truck, we got to—"

But no one waited in the driver's seat. Lyons

looked into the front seat, called out, "Where's Flor?" Panic rose in his throat.

He scanned the street. He saw a door close. The muzzle of a Kalashnikov smashed through a window and fire flashed. Even as he returned fire, Lyons screamed out, "There! They took her in there!"

Fear and reason left Lyons's mind.

12

As the truck hurtled through the streets of East Los Angeles, Abdul Shabaka plotted his next move. The LAYAC produce truck carried all his audiovisual equipment and his entire library of hate films that documented the history of white crimes against blacks and Indians and other non-whites. The film projectors, stereos, audio mixers and video machines would help establish another indoctrination center for young psychopaths and criminals in another city, away from here.

First, he and his squad of personal bodyguards would take shelter in the warehouse he had rented the year before. He'd never put his faith in the LAYAC organization. He only trusted himself. Therefore he had prepared for the day when LAYAC collapsed. He had rented the warehouse, he had modified the building to provide security and defense and had hidden weapons and ammunition inside the building.

But more important, he had a long-distance radio at the warehouse.

With the radio, he would transmit new instructions to his men driving north through Mexico.

Their truck carried another shipment of the drug. Not the few grams Shabaka had left with the gangs in the LAYAC offices, but hundreds of kilos of the chemical.

One kilo of the "crazy dust" created one hundred addicted Warriors of Allah and maintained their need for a month.

One hundred kilos of "crazy dust" created ten thousand fearless, relentless Warriors of Allah who would follow any order, commit any act ordered by their commander, Abdul Shabaka, the Modern Prophet and Leader of the Jihad against the American pigs.

Any crime, any atrocity, any horror.

Ten thousand warriors who knew no fear, who fought despite any wound, who killed without questions, who killed the blue-eyed pigs without mercy.

Ten thousand Warriors of Allah who would lay waste the cities of the white pigs.

SIRENS APPROACHED. The scanner on the front seat of the rented Ford monitored the radio chaos of the approaching squad cars.

Blancanales radioed Detective Towers. "They've got Flor. We're going into the LAYAC offices to get her back."

Lyons interrupted his partner with a shout into the radio. "Warn all those cops on the way, pistols aren't enough. Shotguns and automatic weapons only."

"What're you talking about?" Towers responded. "What's happening there? I thought you were going in quiet."

"Too late for that!" Blancanales barked. "You heard the warning, *compadre*. And tell the other police. Use shotguns and aim for the head. Over."

Lyons slapsealed the Velcro closures of his Kevlar-and-steel trauma-plate battle armor, then buckled on a bandolier of box magazines for his Atchisson. He took up the Atchisson with the fourteen-inch barrel.

Due to the good fortune of the police academy demonstration that morning, the Ford's trunk contained two Atchisson assault shotguns. Blancanales would carry the second full-auto shotgun.

"Got no bandolier for you, Pol," Lyons told Blancanales. "Dump all these extra mags in your pouches."

Blancanales suited up fast. "What are the loads? Double-ought? Jungle mix?"

"Ask Konzaki. He put them all together for the show at the academy. Whatever the loads are, they'll kill punks. Here's the Crowd-killing Device. Gadgets! Ready to go?"

In his battle armor and weapons, Gadgets looked like a walking gun shop. He carried his Uzi and the Uzi he had captured on the roof. He also carried Blancanales's M-16/M-203 hybrid over-and-under assault rifle and grenade launcher. A bandolier of 40mm grenades crossed bandoliers of thirty-round Uzi magazines. He hurried to select grenades from the suitcases he and Blancanales had brought from Stony Man.

"White light shock-stun, right? But no frag or phosphorous?" he said.

"Damn right!" Lyons told him. "Don't want to waste Flor. You ready to go?"

"Here, take these." Gadgets pushed the anti-terrorist grenades on Lyons. Designed to blind and stun airline hijackers without killing passengers, the grenades produced a blinding flash and deafening blast but no shrapnel.

Lyons jammed the grenades in his armor's pouches. He jerked back his Atchisson's actuator to feed the first 12-gauge round. "Time to go! She's in there—"

"She's been in there two minutes," Gadgets said, glancing at his watch. "If she's dead, she's dead. But if we go in there before we're ready, we're dead, too."

"I'm ready now!"

Lyons left the cover of the Ford. A form leaned from a first-floor window to aim an AK. Firing the Atchisson from his hip as he ran, Lyons sprayed the window with a three-blast burst of number two and double-ought steel shot, the high-velocity projectiles raking the window from side to side. The AK gunner's left hand and face disintegrated as the window exploded inward.

Lyons sprinted to the window. Pulling a shock-stun grenade from a thigh pocket, he lobbed it in.

Blancanales ran to the building and waited with

Lyons—both men covering their ears—for the few heartbeats until the grenade's fuse triggered the white flash.

The deafening boom fractured the air. Kicking through the door, Lyons held his Atchisson ready.

In the pale blue light from the side street, he saw a tangle of bodies on the floor. Broken plaster, books, spilled papers covered the semiconscious wounded. He did not see Flor.

Moving fast, Lyons kicked punks over, checking each of them. Blancanales stood in the doorway, his riot-length Atchisson covering the office and the inner door. Lyons pointed to the inner door, shouted, "White light!"

Blancanales aimed at the doorknob and lock. A single round from the 12-gauge removed the entire assembly. Fire from an AK answered. A shock-stun grenade in his hand, Lyons pointed at the center of the door. Blancanales aimed again. Two blasts opened a hole six inches by twelve inches.

Gunners on the other side of the door sprayed wild automatic fire. Lyons let the safety lever flip from the shock-stun, waited to the count of four, then snapped the grenade through the hole in the door.

The blast threw the door across the office. Lyons dodged through the doorway. In the swirling plaster dust, he saw a Chicano sprawled against the wall with a Kalashnikov in his hands. Lyons kicked the Chicano's throat. Through the leather and neoprene of his shoe, he felt the cartilage crush.

Blancanales saw movement on the office floor. A hand lifted an AK by the pistol grip. Whipping around the twenty-inch barrel of his Atchisson, Blancanales jerked the trigger.

Unfamiliar with the assault shotgun, Blancanales inadvertently advanced the fire selector to full-auto as he triggered the blast. The shotgun roared with a burst of point-blank fire.

Andrzej Konzaki, the Stony Man weaponsmith, had loaded that magazine to impress the onlookers of the police academy demonstration with the destructive firepower of the assault weapon. The magazine alternated jungle mix—number two and double-ought steel shot—with slugs. Fired at point-blank distance into a human body, the four rounds, two of steel shot and two of one-ounce slugs, exploded the torso and head, tore through the dying punk in a storm of projectiles to strike the linoleum-and-concrete-slab floor of the office, and finally ricocheted, spraying high-velocity steel and lead fragments in all directions.

Gore splashed the office. Konzaki's weapon and ammunition succeeded in highly impressing Rosario Blancanales, ex-Green Beret and veteran of several wars. For a moment he stared at the mass of glistening meat and blood that had been a body. He had never seen an infantry weapon—other than a grenade launcher or a LAAW rocket—create such mayhem. He dropped out the empty magazine and jammed in another.

In the corridor, Lyons kicked over gasping,

bleeding gang boys. One had a Kalashnikov, another an M-16, a third a .38 pistol. Lyons went flat against the wall and peered through the dust that grayed the corridor.

The corridor led through the old apartment buildings, passing from one building to the next, connecting offices and meeting rooms. Several doors opened onto it.

A form dashed from an office. Lyons raised his Atchisson, but Blancanales fired first, a blast of steel shot throwing the punk down. Lyons looked to Blancanales and raised a shock-stun grenade in his hand. Blancanales nodded. He braced his Atchisson to cover his partner.

Lyons ran forward, one shoulder against the wall, his eyes searching the doorways for any movement. At the first doorway, as the wounded punk tried to rise on shattered, blood-spurting legs, Lyons tossed the shock-stun inside.

With a growl, a wide-eyed punk stomped from the office, his M-16 spraying fire. Lyons stayed to the side and slammed his arm down on the weapon's barrel and black plastic foregrip. Slugs from the M-16 killed the wounded punk on the floor, then the blastflash of the grenade threw the hyped-up homeboy across the corridor. Lyons snatched the pistol grip of his slung Atchisson and pointed the fourteen-inch barrel at the punk's head. When the muzzle flashed, the head ceased to exist.

Looking into the office, Lyons saw a form thrashing in the clutter of spilled papers and books. The young black man wore a black jacket vivid with the gang logo, The Headhunters, and a severed head dripping blood. Glitter made the staring eyes of the head sparkle. The gang punk reached for a weapon.

Lyons stomped on the Headhunter's hand, breaking the wrist under his heel. The punk snatched at a pistol with his left hand.

The heel of Lyons's shoe came down again, this time on the punk's solar plexus. Though the stomp propelled the air from the teenager's lungs, he did not feel the pain. His hand closed around the pistol grip. Lyons kicked the pistol away.

Lyons put the muzzle of the Atchisson into the soft hollow of the punk's throat, where his neck met his collarbones and chest. Lyons asked one question, "Where's the woman?"

The Headhunter sucked down a breath and attacked Lyons, flailing at him with his broken hand and his good fist. Lyons pushed the muzzle into the punk's throat. "Where's the woman?"

Clawing at Lyons, the punk thrashed against the muzzle of the full-auto shotgun. Lurching from the floor, the punk grabbed at Lyons's right hand gripping the Atchisson.

The blast sent the Headhunter into the void to forever hunt for his head.

The torso flopped and quivered on the floor as Lyons went to the door. He took another shock-stun from his battle armor's pouches.

"They're rushing—" Blancanales called out,

the booming of his Atchisson cutting his words short.

A storm of autofire swept the corridor. Five-point-fifty-six-millimeter and 7.62 ComBloc slugs ricocheted and whined from the walls and floors as Blancanales sprayed the line of onrushing gang punks with his Atchisson.

The shock of a bullet impact knocked Blancanales back. Lyons saw his partner fall, once more called out, "White light!"

Throwing the shock-stun grenade at the mob of punks, Lyons jerked another seven-round magazine from his bandolier. Holding his Atchisson in one hand, he shielded his left ear with his other hand and turned away.

The boom-flash silenced the autorifles for an instant. His head ringing, Lyons leaned from the protection of the doorway and emptied his Atchisson into the downed crowd of chemically hyped punks.

High-velocity steel exploded skulls, ripped away arms and feet. Lyons took cover again, dropped out the empty mag, jammed in the next. He flipped the fire selector up to semiauto and searched for targets.

A punk in a blood-splashed purple jacket rose to his knees. He swung a Kalashnikov to his shoulder as Lyons put fifty steel balls through his chest at 1400 feet per second.

Another Chicano clawed his way from under a dead comrade and pointed a .45 automatic. High-velocity steel ripped away his arm and head.

A wounded punk pushed himself up from the bloody floor. He lurched upright and swung a machete. Lyons set the Atchisson's sight on the teenager's forehead. Brains sprayed.

Lyons pulled another magazine out of his gear, then went to Blancanales's side. The stocky Puerto Rican got to his feet. He looked to his battle armor. A bullet had torn through the Kevlar to punch through an Atchisson magazine. But the steel trauma plate had finally stopped the slug.

Blancanales gave Lyons a thumbs-up. But when he tried to reload his Atchisson, he found the lower receiver deformed by a bullet. A ComBloc slug had punched through the magazine well and smashed the interior mechanisms.

Another gang surged into the corridor. Lyons raised his Atchisson and rushed them, firing from the hip, every blast from the 12-gauge assault shotgun slamming a crazed punk back.

Slinging the inoperative Atchisson over his shoulder, Blancanales grabbed a blood-slick Kalashnikov from the floor. He went to Lyons's side, firing two- and three-shot bursts into the shoulder-to-shoulder mass of teenage monsters.

Lyons's weapon went empty. He knelt on one knee to reload. He dropped out the spent magazine and jammed in the next. But the magazine did not snap into the weapon. Lyons pushed it but felt no snap that would indicate correct seating. Pulling out the mag, he saw flesh and a bit of bone fouling the top 12-gauge shell.

As Lyons struggled to clean the fouled magazine and reload the Atchisson, Blancanales saw one punk charge ahead, a machete raised high. Snap-sighting on the rabid teenager's chest, Blancanales fired. A single round staggered the punk, but he did not fall. The Kalashnikov rifle empty, Blancanales saw the punk continuing forward, the machete still raised high.

Blancanales took the captured Kalashnikov by the barrel and rushed the oncoming punk. With all his strength, Blancanales swung the rifle.

The blow crushed the punk's skull. But the spot-welds joining the cheap pot-metal components of the ComBloc weapon broke. Left with only the Kalashnikov's barrel in his hands, Blancanales looked for another weapon as a second punk came at them with a revolver flashing.

A .38 slug ripped past his ear as Blancanales grabbed a machete from the corridor's gore-splashed floor. Then Lyons's Atchisson boomed. The punk with the pistol fell. But the wall of drug-crazed blood-lusting human animals did not stop.

"Down!" Gadgets screamed to his partners.

Falling to their faces in the blood, Lyons and Blancanales heard the M-203 grenade launcher fire.

The first two punks lurched as a blast of twenty-seven double-ought balls slammed into them. But the low-velocity projectiles from a 40mm buckshot round did not stop them. Blood spurting from their faces and chests, their comrades pushing the dying punks forward, they continued on.

Lyons fired his Atchisson as a continuous line of 9mm slugs ripped into the mob. Gadgets fired an Uzi in each hand, holding the triggers back, brass raining around him. Finally, the Israeli submachine guns went silent.

From his prone position, Lyons saw an M-16 rising. He did not aim. He fired wild, saw blood spray the ceiling. Then his weapon's action locked back.

Punks still came. Blancanales rose to one knee. He had picked up a machete. He slashed with it. A punk's hand and pistol hit the wall. Another pointed a shotgun and fired, but the blast went into the back of the one-handed punk.

Intestines exploded. Blancanales pushed the dying punk aside and hacked again and again as the shotgunner pumped the Remington's slide.

The arms and shotgun fell. The maimed punk thrashed at Blancanales with the stumps of his arms. Then Lyons shoved his partner aside and put the muzzle of the fourteen-inch barrel of the Atchisson under the screaming gang boy's chin.

Blast flipped the corpse backward. Lyons semiautoed blasts into another running punk, then killed the crawling wounded.

Blood-soaked, flesh glistening on their battle armor, the three men of Able Team remained alive in the corridor of slaughter.

Gadgets splashed through the blood to his partners. The reloaded Uzis swung from his shoulders.

He gripped the M-16/M-203. Eyes wide with horror, his breath coming in panic pants, Gadgets kept repeating, "This is heavy, this is heavy, I mean, I came to the party late, and I don't know about this scene. Definitely number one thousand. Maybe one million."

"If they rush us again," Blancanales told Lyons, "we are overrun."

Lyons slammed another magazine into his Atchisson. "We haven't found Flor."

They heard footsteps and the firing of shotguns and pistols. Lyons looked to his partners.

"Here they come...."

13

As black-and-white units screeched to tire-smoking stops in front of the apartments, Detective Bill Towers assembled the police officers into improvised fire-teams. Though the department had issued additional shotguns to the units patrolling the city, not every officer had one of the riot weapons.

Towers took Lyons's warning seriously. If that ex-cop said the men needed shotguns and automatic weapons, Towers knew Lyons meant it.

An incident immediately proved Lyons's warning true.

As Towers sent a two-man unit to the side street with an order to seal off the side exits and the alley, the officer behind the steering wheel called out, "Behind you!"

Turning, Towers saw a teenager in jeans, sneakers and a gang jacket run from the front door of the ground floor LAYAC offices. The teenager held a machete high as he sprinted for Towers, screaming hate jargon, "Die, you white genocidal Nazi running dog!"

"Halt or I'll fire!" Towers shouted out as he

pulled his .38 pistol loaded with department-approved solid-point ammunition. "Halt—"

The command did not stop the punk. Towers sighted over the four-inch barrel of his Smith & Wesson and double-actioned six slugs into the punk's chest.

The slugs did not stop the youth. Blood spurting from his chest, he crossed the sidewalk and street in a few steps. He swung the machete at Towers. Towers sidestepped.

As the machete skipped off the sheet metal of the black-and-white, the officer in the driver's seat fired his service revolver point-blank into the gut of the punk. Slugs exited the punk's back and broke the plate-glass windows of the LAYAC offices.

But the punk did not fall. Retreating from the bloody teenage psychopath, Towers pulled the backup pistol he carried—in violation of department regulations—in a holster at the small of his back: a Colt Commander. Loaded with hollow-points—again in violation of department policy—the large-caliber autopistol went on line with the punk's chest as he rushed to kill Towers.

Towers snapped two shots. The first hollow-point slammed the punk back, exploding through his chest to destroy his heart and the knot of arteries between the lungs. The second slug went high and struck the dying punk in the nose. His head exploded with the shock-force of the impact.

Even when the medically dead zombie finally fell, the legs and arms continued to thrash, the machete still gripped in its right fist, the metal of the blade clanking and sparking on the asphalt as if the punk's arm had a nervous system independent of the destroyed brain.

Towers stared down at the thrashing corpse, astounded. Officers from other cars ran to the corpse. The driver of the squad car announced in a shaky voice, "Holy shit! You saw it. Towers put six through the chest. I put another four through its gut. And it still took two forty-fives to put it down!"

"Everyone with a shotgun over here!" Towers yelled, assembling officers.

As they gathered, Towers continued directing black-and-white units to surround the apartments. Inside, the battle continued. Directing his men, Towers heard the hammering of autofire, the booming of shotguns inside the buildings. He addressed the officers around him. "There're three men fighting in there. The crazies captured an officer and those three men went in to save the officer. We're going in to help. Everyone got their pockets full of ammo?"

"We shoot to kill?" an officer called out. "Do we try to arrest them?"

"This is war!" Towers shouted back. "Look at that one in the street and tell me if you're going to read them their rights!"

The group rushed into the battle.

MONITORING THE POLICE COMMUNICATIONS on their scanner, reporter Mark Lannon and his technicians sped to the battle at the LAYAC offices. When the sound man driving the van saw the flashing lights of the police cars blocking the avenue, he swerved onto a side street.

"I'll circle around and try the alley," the sound man told Lannon.

"Do it. Get past those pigs. We'll put this on the morning news. Smear those Nazi pigs."

They wove through the side streets, down one street, then two right turns, finally approaching on a tree-darkened street where no police squad cars parked. Lannon directed his crew with whispers. "Get the equipment together. We're going to sneak in there. If they see us, they'll pull some pigshit jive about the scene of a crime or whatever. Once we got the pictures, they can only subpoena the tapes."

"Right on!" the cameraman agreed.

After checking their video gear and sound-recording equipment, the three newsmen slipped into the shadows. They heard intermittent gunfire as they neared the alley behind the LAYAC buildings.

Headlights swept from the avenue. The three counterculture activists hurried into the darkness beside a trash dumpster. When Lannon saw two uniformed officers setting out flares to halt all traffic, he said to his cameraman, "Get some tape of that!"

Then he turned to his sound recordist. "Get all the noise and shooting. Maybe we can loop and dub it later on, make it sound like World War III."

A furious exchange of fire somewhere inside the building startled them. The sound man turned on his deck and held out a microphone to the sound of the firefight. "Won't need to overdub *that* . . . ."

Another set of headlights flashed, this time in the alley. Lannon saw a lowered Chevy boulevard cruiser turn from one of the garages. He slapped the shoulders of his technicians. "There's some of the LAYAC brothers. We'll do an interview with them. Get some real shit on the pigs."

Stepping from the concealing shadows, Lannon waved his arms for the Chevy to stop. His technicians took their places in the alley. The cameraman switched on his sungun spotlight, the sound recordist extended a long microphone.

"Hey, comrades!" Lannon called out. "What's happening in there? We're from K-Marx. What's the truth?"

The Chevy stopped. Going to the driver's window, Lannon leaned in. What he saw sent him quickly staggering back.

A gang punk with a demented grin waved a sawed-off double-barreled shotgun at him. The punk lowered his aim and fired.

At a distance of ten feet, the spray of birdshot destroyed Mark Lannon's legs. In a tangle of shattered bones and muscle sinew, Lannon sat on the alley's asphalt. He watched as the Chevy's doors flew open. Punks crowded from the doors, machetes and pistols and automatic rifles in their hands.

Dropping his video gear, the cameraman ran. A burst of AK fire killed him. The sound man put up his hands in surrender. Several punks advanced on him while the others went to Lannon.

"I'm with you, I'm a comrade in struggle," the sound man pleaded, tears running down his bushy beard. "Here's my Communist Party card. I'm with you. I'll show you my card, I'm a paid-up member of the—"

As he reached for his wallet, a punk stepped forward and chopped off the sound man's arm with a machete. The sound man's face contorted with a scream that only rattled in his throat.

Machetes and pistols and point-blank gunfire dismembered the Communist sound man.

Mark Lannon suffered longer. With his white skin, stylish hair and neatly trimmed mustache, the reporter personified the typical bourgeois white man to the drug-enraged crowd of young black and Chicano gang boys.

Machetes flashed in the dark alley. First, the punks cut away Lannon's shattered legs. Then his fingers and hands. As the white man's screams echoed in the filthy corridor behind the buildings, the punks methodically reduced him to a flopping torso with a screaming head.

Cross fire of shotguns and department-approved .38 pistols drove the street gang back to their vehicle. Bleeding, their throats filling with blood even as they screamed defiance at the officers, the punks attempted to escape in their supercharged Chevy.

Officers fired shotguns and rifles into the engine, point-blank into the driver's head, then at the rear tires. The Chevy careered across the side street and into a tree.

Flames exploded. Orange light from the rising flames lighted the alley. Then the officers found the dead cameraman and the butchered sound recordist.

A wailing cry lead them to the thing lying in blood and a clutter of human parts. Only when they saw the arms and legs did the officers realize the flopping, bleeding meat had been a human being.

After another few seconds of pain and blind, silent anguish, Mark Lannon, the K-Marx man of the people, The Voice of Socialist Truth, finally went silent.

STORMING THROUGH THE OFFICES and hallways of the LAYAC complex, Towers and his men killed everything that moved. There seemed to be no end to the punks in the building. They came from doorways, they came down the stairs, they rose from the heaps of dead to fight again. This was the crucial battle.

Towers rushed through one doorway and fell flat, expecting autofire. But he heard only the gunfire in the other rooms. Scrambling over the floor, he scanned the large room.

Black Nationalist posters plastered one wall. The three other walls had been painted stark white. He could not understand the purpose of the white walls until he saw the projection ports.

The room had been a theater with multiple projectors. Marks on the wall indicated mountings for now-gone speakers for a total-surround sound system. Wires and cables dangled from conduits around the walls.

His examination of the theater was interrupted by firing outside the door. Bracing his Colt Commander in both hands, Towers waited for a gang to appear. He heard a voice call out, "Police! Freeze, whoever you are!"

"We're on your side!"

"You're the Federals?"

"That's us—the Super-Feds. . . ."

Towers recognized the voice of the Wizard, the electronics specialist who worked with Carl Lyons. He went to the door and announced himself. "Detective Towers coming out!"

Only then did he emerge. He saw the three men with automatic weapons and military gear standing with a group of his uniformed officers. He could not identify Lyons.

Blood crusted all three men. Blood concealed their features and hair color. Finally, Towers heard a voice that identified his ex-partner. "What about the woman? Any of you see her?"

"No," Towers told Lyons. "We came in through the front. Where were you?"

"We went in through the side. There's a first-floor hallway connecting all this together. We got hit by banzai charges of scumbags."

"Yeah, tell us about it. We met a few of them ourselves."

The blood-masked man that Towers could recognize only by voice stared urgently at him. "Flor has to be somewhere. We've got to search every room in this place. Did any of them get away? Other than that one truck?"

"Could they have her in the truck?" Towers asked.

"No chance," another of the Able Team soldiers answered. Towers recognized the sonorous voice as the voice of Lyons's Puerto Rican partner. "That truck went *muy rápido*. They wouldn't have taken the time to grab her. And I don't think they could have grabbed her. Not without leaving bodies."

An officer returned from checking the corridor. He said nothing.

"So what's down there?" one of the other officers demanded of him.

The officer lifted one of his feet and pointed at it. Blood glistened on his shoe. He had stepped in blood deeper than his shoe tops. "Does that tell you what's down there?"

As other cops went to stare at the carnage, Lyons called them back. "We're still looking for our partner. We got to find her."

"Sure, bad man, we're on it." Towers spoke into his walkie-talkie and directed his other officers to check every room and hallway. "If we don't find her here, we'll question the headman of LAYAC. We grabbed him down in the marina. He tried to get away in his yacht."

An officer reported. "We got civilians coming down the fire escapes. There're apartments up there that have got nothing to do with the gangs."

"Well, help them down. 'Protect and serve,' officer. Get to it."

As the three men of Able Team started for the avenue, Towers spoke into his walkie-talkie again. "We got three Federals coming out. Do the city a favor and hose them off before they get in one of our cars."

14

Flor Trujillo rode on the bumper of the five-ton truck speeding from East Los Angeles. The wind whipping her hair, she gripped the latch of the roll-up aluminum cargo door.

As her hands became tired, every bump and lurch threatened her with a high-speed encounter with asphalt. She watched for a police car, hoping to signal for assistance.

But the only patrol cars she saw flashed past in the opposite direction. Lights flashing, sirens screaming, the black-and-white units went to help the officers caught in the ambush she had overheard on the scanner.

So she held on. Few other cars traveled the streets and boulevards of the city. She saw the driver of one car do a double take at the sight of her—a young Hispanic woman in a wind-flagged green dress and high heels—riding the cargo truck's bumper.

Then the truck went onto the freeway. Gripping the latch, she eased herself into a crouch as the evening air tore at her hair and skirt. Behind her, she saw only two or three distant pairs of headlights. On this night after the slaughter of the Valencia family, no one risked the freeways.

A few minutes before, she had seen the truck swerve from the alley behind the LAYAC building. The truck had lurched for a moment as the driver clashed the gears. On impulse, she dashed from the rented Ford and stepped up on the bumper. She wished she had taken a hand-radio. With only her Detonics and a few extra magazines, she sped to a destination unknown.

She felt movement inside the truck. Pressing her ear against the roll-up aluminum, she heard voices and footsteps. The vibrations and noises of the speeding truck made the words incomprehensible. But now she knew she faced more opponents than only the driver and the gunman in the truck's cab.

Without slowing, the truck swerved onto an off ramp. The truck's body clattered and shook as the tires seized the asphalt, the acrid smoke of burning rubber swirling around Flor. The truck whipped through a right turn, then accelerated again.

Before Flor could catch sight of a boulevard street sign, the truck whipped through another right turn and sped through a gray district of wrecking yards and industrial buildings. She saw only empty streets and desolate parking lots under the blue white light of the mercury-arc streetlamps.

Finally the truck slowed. Flor heard the cab door open and footsteps run from the truck to the building. Steel clanked against a steel door.

Now came the danger. She knew she must some-how slip away from the truck without betraying herself. In the isolation of a manufacturing area, with only her autopistol against the rifles of the gang punks who guarded the truck, she had no doubt of the outcome of a pursuit and firefight.

She peered around the side of the truck. She snapped her head back instantly when she saw the punk at the warehouse door looking at the truck. The truck lurched into motion and turned to enter the warehouse.

Desperate, Flor considered her options.

Run and be seen and pursued.

Stay on the bumper and be seen as she rode into the garage.

She could not run, and she could not remain im-mobile. Her desperation forced her into the only possible action. . . .

Gripping the edge of the bumper with one down-stretched hand, she released her other hand's grip on the latch. Then she grabbed the bumper with both hands, and thrust a foot under-neath it.

She hung below the bumper by her hands and one foot, her back only inches from the asphalt. Reaching into the undercarriage of the truck, she gripped the gritty steel of the chassis. She lost her high-heeled shoe as she struggled to maintain her toehold. She let her other shoe fall away as she moved her other leg.

The truck paused. Hanging underneath the

truck, she heard the punk at the garage door shout out, *"A la derecha. Poquito a la derecha."*

With a lurch, the truck continued into the warehouse. She heard the steel door crash down. The punk jumped onto the bumper and released the truck's cargo latch.

Footsteps and voices inside the truck became feet and legs as a gang crowded out from it. She heard ghetto English and Spanish. Another voice spoke in softly accented English. Flor could not identify the accent as the man talked.

"To your positions, my warriors. Though we will be secure here, we must remain on guard. Soon we go to another city and continue Allah's work."

The punks answered. "Sure thing, brother.... Waste those white devils."

Hanging by her hands and ankles, Flor waited for the gang to disperse. Only after the footsteps of the punks and their leaders receded did she ease herself down to the oily concrete of the warehouse floor. Crawling a few feet, she pressed herself against the double tires for concealment. She watched the activity in the warehouse.

Work lights in the high ceiling lighted the interior. The driver had parked the truck in the center of the building. Open concrete extended on all sides. A few boxes and crates and tables lined the walls. But she saw no open doors. Flor could not hope to snake from under the truck and dash out to the street.

The truck had carried her into a trap.

She could do nothing but wait.

Across the concrete space, she saw a stoop-shouldered black man in a dark blue suit. He wore his hair conservatively short. Glasses framed in black plastic gave him the look of an accountant. He directed two gang punks in blue nylon jackets and dirty jeans to open a wooden crate.

The punks crowbarred away the crate's lid. They carefully lifted out a block of Styrofoam and put it on a table. Then the black man took a knife from the punks and cut the tape that secured the Styrofoam.

When the packaging fell away, Flor saw a short-wave radio. The black man attached antenna leads to the back of the radio and handed a coil of wire to one of the punks. The punk took the wire up a flight of stairs to the roof. The other youth ran an extension cord to the radio.

Hiding only a few steps away, Flor heard every word the black man said.

"This is Shabaka. Calling the truck. Shabaka calling the truck...."

The black man repeated his call for minutes. Finally a voice responded. The monotonic, strangely disembodied voice alerted Flor to the electronic code guarding the conversation.

Like the hand-radios Able Team used, the long-distance radio employed encoding circuits to electronically scramble and unscramble every conversation. Only those with the radio sets could understand the transmissions. Any technician or amateur radio enthusiast monitoring the transmissions would hear only bursts of static.

"This is the truck," came the reply. "We're a hundred miles south of the border. No problems, we're making good time."

"The Los Angeles delivery is canceled."

"What?"

"The Los Angeles delivery is canceled. We will take the delivery in Escondido instead. Do you understand?"

"It won't be going to L.A. We're going to drop it Escondido instead."

"This address is outside of the city. Are you ready to copy down the address?"

"Right. I got a pencil. Go ahead."

Flor memorized the address and the time of the delivery as Shabaka dictated it to his truck crew Shabaka switched off the radio.

As the punks put the radio in the truck above her, Flor racked her imagination for a way to escape. With the information on the place and time of the delivery, Able Team had the opportunity to follow the conspiracy to its source. Whatever the cargo—weapons, terrorists, cash or drugs—the cargo and drivers and truck would provide another lead in breaking the puzzle of the gang siege that terrorized Los Angeles.

But Flor knew she must escape silently, secretly. If Shabaka suspected he had been overheard by a federal agent, he would change the location of the delivery.

How could she escape? She had seen the punks lock both the big cargo door and the office door.

If she left the darkness under the truck, she risked an instant firefight.

If she stayed under the truck and waited, she chanced the punks discovering her.

Flor decided to take the greatest risk, to wait until the punks and their leader left the garage, then drop away from the truck when the opportunity came.

She prayed that the truck would slow for a moment at some point on the route to the town on the Mexican border. Hitting the asphalt at a high speed would not be pleasant....

A voice interrupted her thoughts.

"What's that under the truck?" one punk asked another.

A Kalashnikov rifle gripped in his right hand, a black punk got down on his hands and knees to peer under the cargo truck.

Flor shot him in the face. She scrambled from under the truck and grabbed the AK from his still-twitching hand. Snapping down the safety lever to semiauto, Flor put a single shot through the chest of the other punk as he struggled to unsling the AK on his shoulder.

A brown-skinned youth ran down the stairs. Flor put a ComBloc slug through the center of his chest.

Running around the truck, she came face to face with another Chicano punk. Without raising the Kalashnikov in her hands, she jerked the trigger twice, the first slug smashing through his crotch, the second slug striking him in the top of his head as he doubled over in agony.

Without the strange drug supplied by Shabaka, the punks knew fear. They struggled to aim their rifles with shaking hands as a barefooted young woman in a shimmering dress ran through their midst, killing them.

A sentry at the door turned at the sound of the shots and raised his rifle. He saw the woman with the Kalashnikov. Sighting, he fired his M-16.

Another punk chose that moment to rush the woman. Swinging a machete, he attacked. Flor blocked the blade with the barrel of the Soviet autorifle, then the punk's head exploded with the impact of a 5.56mm slug.

Dodging from the mist of brains and blood, Flor saw another youth rushing her. She threw herself sideways, felt her shoulder hit a truck tire. A blast deafened her and showered her with chips of enamel paint from the truck. Kicking out, she tripped the charging punk.

Flor extended the rifle with one hand. With the muzzle against his face, she fired. The flash illuminated an expression of surprise and confusion as the slug smashed through the youth's eye socket.

Rolling, she gained the cover of a few crates and cardboard boxes against one wall. She shoved through the boxes as slugs pocked the wall around her.

She clicked the Kalashnikov's fire selector down to full-auto and sighted on a muzzle-flash. A burst sent a punk staggering backward.

A dead guy sprawled only an arm's reach away. Flor grabbed his shirt and pulled him into the boxes. From the corpse, she took a web belt hung with AK mags and a .357 Magnum pistol. She took one of the magazines out and held it ready as she searched for targets.

She recognized the voice of the black man, Shabaka. "All of you. Fire there," she heard. "All at once. She's in there."

Spraying slugs at the voice, she dived through cardboard, felt her shoulder hit a heavy crate. Autofire punched the walls and concrete floor as the surviving punks tried to kill her with wild, unaimed bursts.

She took cover behind the heavy crate and waited. She felt several slugs hit the crate, but the two-by-fours and the contents stopped the slugs. She waited, silent, not moving.

"Manuel," Shabaka called out again. "Go take a look."

"Let's shoot her some more first," Manuel answered, then emptied another magazine into the clutter of boxes. Slugs ricocheted and fragmented on the concrete.

Flor felt high-velocity metal rip through one of her legs. But she did not cry out or move, not even as the blood flowed and the pain came. She waited. As the shooting continued, she dropped out the AK's magazine and put in the full magazine with thirty rounds. Counting the one round in the chamber of the AK, she had thirty-one shots.

Then she checked her wound. With her fingers, she found where a tiny bit of metal had hit her leg. Exhaling hard against the pain, she pressed on her flesh and felt the piece of metal in her leg. She would not let the injury slow her.

Shotgun blasts threw cardboard and bits of wood everywhere. Finally, Shabaka stopped the barrage. "She's dead! Now get the body and find out who she was."

The punks searched for her.

Alone on the killing floor, with the rifles of the gang poised ready to take her life away, Flor waited.

15

At a hundred miles an hour on the deserted free-ways, Detective Towers raced to the command center of the joint LAPD, state and federal task force of officers assembled to fight the gang punks terrorizing Los Angeles. He spoke to Able Team in the car as he drove.

"We got Silva cold. Read him his rights, served the warrant, took the evidence. Perfect case."

"What about interrogation?" Lyons had rinsed off some of the gore from the LAYAC slaughter-fest, but blood still obstinately clung to his hair and the hair of his arms. His luggage in the trunk of the rented Ford had provided clean shirts for himself and his partners.

"They're questioning him, but no answers yet."

"What're they doing?" Lyons demanded. "Letting him discuss his case with his legal staff? While those monsters rip Flor Trujillo apart?"

"You still think they've got her?"

Blancanales leaned forward from the back seat. "Lyons, the ones in that truck didn't grab her. Maybe some other gang—"

Lyons interrupted his partner. His desperate

worry for the woman he loved did not allow anyone to reason with him. "I figure they somehow
got her into that truck. And I figure Silva will
know where the truck went. That's all we've got to
go on."

"Makes sense to me...." Towers agreed.

"You weren't there," Blancanales told him.

Slowing to sixty miles an hour, Towers left the
freeway. He sideslipped through a screaming,
two-wheeled left-hand turn, then accelerated. He
switched on the siren at the intersections.

In the back seat, Gadgets looked at the boulevard flashing past. "You cops, you drive crazy."
He put his hands over his eyes. "Tell me when it's
safe to look."

Turning to Gadgets and Blancanales, Towers
steered with one hand. "It's part of the benefits
package. You can't expect men to go out and face
the puke of the world for the pay of a nursery-
school teacher. So they give us some perks. Like
supercharged Dodges."

"Please," Blancanales asked. "At this speed, it
is important that you watch the road."

"What road?" Towers questioned them, his
face solemn. "This is a jet plane!"

As the Dodge hurtled through an intersection, it
hit a dip where the boulevards crossed. The undercarriage smashed into the asphalt, then the car left
the pavement at ninety miles an hour.

"Whoooeeeee!" Towers laughed. "Air-
borne—"

The Dodge smashed its undercarriage again when it landed. Towers fought the wheel as the heavy sedan drifted sideways. A sign in the center of the boulevard flew end over end into the night sky after the Dodge sheared off its four-by-four post. Finally, Towers returned the speeding car to a straight line. Still laughing, he floored the accelerator. Lyons punched him in the shoulder.

"Get serious, will you? This is no time to show off."

"Never had a better opportunity. All the good, decent citizens are at home snorting cocaine and watching the LAPD storm troopers stomping on the civil liberties of the vatos and Crips. In living color. In stereo. In wide-screen video...."

Slowing, Towers swerved into a parking lot. The LAPD had taken over a high school closed for summer vacation. The parking lots provided assembly areas for the officers and vehicles. Typewriters and papers could be seen covering tables in the gymnasium. The school's many telephone lines provided quick communication to all the law-enforcement offices participating in the counterattack.

Blancanales saw the parked squad cars and unmarked federal vehicles. He shook Gadgets. "You can look now. We got here alive."

"This car stinks of blood," Towers told Able Team as he parked at the end of the lot. They all got out. "There's showers in the gym. Why don't you guys have a proper cleanup?"

"No time," Lyons answered. "Where's Silva?"

"Okay, come on. Maybe all the blood will enhance your impact as an interrogator."

Uniformed LAPD officers with shotguns and M-16s guarded a side entrance to the gymnasium. Lyons laughed bitterly as he passed the guards.

"Where were they when the punks rushed us?"

Towers turned to Lyons. "Those men aren't watching for punks. They're protecting us from the media and the Civil Liberties Union."

"I believe it."

"Silva's down this way."

A group of men in suits stood at the end of a row of lockers. A screen identified a small room as the towel room. One of the plainclothesmen saw Towers and the three bloodied Federals. He grabbed a briefcase from the floor and rushed to them.

"I've got information for you and...these specialists," the young man in a suit told Towers.

At first, Towers did not recognize the man. "Oh, yeah. You're not LAPD. You're that liaison man for the Olympics antiterrorist detail. Why are you on this program?"

"The incidents last night qualified as terrorism."

"Sure did. What's this information?"

"The People's Republic of Cuba has decided to cooperate in the prosecution of Mr. Mario Silva."

"The Cubans?" Lyons asked, incredulous.

"Here's a copy." The liaison man passed Lyons

a thick folder. "Most of it's in Spanish. Some of the papers are in English. Even some Russian and French. Silva has been a long-term agent for Communist Cuba—very surprising when you consider his family background. His father was a close associate of Generalissimo Batista. The Dirección General de Inteligencia assigned him to create a network of organizations and individuals who would advance Cuban interests in the United States. And he received millions of dollars to fund his operation.

"However, Mr. Silva used much of the money to finance drug deals. He kept the profits for himself. Seems they discovered his role in this terrorism and they want none of the responsibility. The Cuban consulate in New York said they'd send some intelligence officers out to testify if there's a trial. How's that for cooperation?"

"*If* there's a trial?" Blancanales asked. "Why the if?"

"Sometimes these things never go to trial," the liaison man answered. "Too public."

"Thanks a lot," Lyons said to him. "I got a good idea of my approach on the interrogation."

"Also, there's other information. Specifically for you three gentlemen. From an individual named Kurtzman. It's on a cassette. He said he couldn't wait for a transcontinental courier, so I recorded the encoded information over the phone. He said the Wizard would know what to do."

The three men of Able Team glanced at one another. Kurtzman, the Stony Man intelligence and computer specialist, must have been very hard-pressed to trust an outsider even with code names.

"Where's the cassette?" Blancanales asked.

"Here." The liaison man passed him a minia-ture cassette deck. "You can keep the cassette. But the tape recorder's mine."

"We'll only need it for a few minutes," Gadgets told him. He pushed the playback button. Elec-tronic hiss came from the tiny built-in speaker on the expensive unit, the most expensive and sophis-ticated on the civilian market. "Supercool. Stereo static."

They moved to the towel room, making their way through the knot of plainclothesmen. The uniformed officer blocking the door recognized Towers and Able Team and opened the door with-out a word.

The towel room was actually several rooms. There were storage rooms for clean and used towels. Another room bore a stenciled red cross and the words First Aid. The interrogators had Mario Silva in the used-towel room.

Seated in a straight-back school chair, Silva smoked a cigarette and stared into space, bored by the questions from the three police officers inter-rogating him.

"Before we go in—" Gadgets stopped Lyons and Blancanales "—we decode this. Pol. Take the tape player, play it into your hand-radio while we listen on my radio."

Able Team went to the far side of the towel room to play the tape. The circuits of the radios decoded the noise on the tape. Kurtzman's resynthesized, monotonic voice hissed from Gadgets's radio. "Just got this info. Very top secret. As you'd say, Gadgets, Cosmic Top Secret.

"I scanned all Stony Man data on drugs. Found an unconfirmed report. An ex-Green Beret came out of Libya. Said he'd made a deal to smuggle some kind of new 'crazy dust'—a drug that made soldiers go crazy—into the United States with a Saudi Arabian prince. The smuggler said he'd gone to Khaddafi Duck Himself with the scheme. Ended up supplying it on contract to an ex-Panther, ex-Death's Angel named Shabaka. That's the only name he got.

"I put it through the machines. Nothing. I talked to Konzaki about all this, and he told me you guys have got more than freaked-out street punks to watch out for. You understand? Watch out for crew cuts in suits. And don't trust anyone with a Harvard accent. Over and out."

Gadgets clicked off the radios and tape player. "Oh, wow. Very curious."

Lyons looked toward the room where Silva sat. "It'd be interesting to find out who the Saudi Arabian prince actually worked for, but we've got other work to do. After we find Flor, we'll call the White House."

"You're talking totally crazy," Gadgets said.

"After I saw Unomundo's hired generals and

colonels rubbing bellies with United States senators," Lyons said, "I decided I'd never know exactly what was going on. In fact, maybe even Cuba knows something about this that we don't. Now no more talk."

Rushing over to the used-towel room, Lyons stood in the doorway and studied Silva. A wide-shouldered Hispanic with perfectly styled hair and an expensive suit, Silva had never worked with his hands or struggled or fought. His manikin-perfect face had no scars or worry lines.

Silva looked up at the man filling the doorway. He saw polyester slacks stained with filth and crusted blood. The man wore a freshly laundered shirt—the front still had the creases from a suitcase—but blood stained his hands and arms. Bits of blood clotted in his hair. As Silva studied the blond stranger, he became aware of a new smell in the room.

The smell of blood and cordite and death.

Absently Lyons rolled the thick folder in his hands, gripped it and slapped it like a length of pipe in his left palm. Voices stopped. The steady whap-whap-whap of the roll of papers became the only sound in the small concrete-walled room. Finally, Lyons spoke to the plainclothes interrogators.

"Officers, *we* will question the prisoner now. Please leave us alone with him. And don't interrupt us."

The plainclothes officers grinned to one another. But Towers shook his head. "We're responsible for what the prisoner looks like and I can't let—"

Lyons crouched, balancing on the balls of his feet in front of Silva. He looked into the man's face and smiled. "This *puto*—" Lyons used the Mexican word for a male whore "—is only a coward and a worm. He will answer all our questions."

Towers motioned the interrogators out. The men laughed as they left. The last man closed the door. Silva twisted his face into a sneer.

"I'll be free tomorrow. And I'll file a lawsuit claiming defamation of character. That obscenity will cost you millions of dollars."

Lyons ignored Silva's words. "Your father and his friends fought Castro. Your family fled Cuba. If you don't answer every question we ask, photocopies of this go to your father, your father's friends, every anti-Castro organization in the country, and Omega Seven."

Opening the curled folder, Lyons showed Silva the first page of the Cuban dossier. Full-face and profile photos identified Mario Silva. The stamp of the Dirección General de Inteligencia marked the lower right-hand corner of the identification sheet.

Silva went white. Lyons fanned through the dossier, showing the young attorney the hundreds of photocopied documents condemning him to prison and lifelong exile from his family and the Cuban American community.

Lyons grinned. "You'll talk now?"

Silva tried to speak. But his mouth had gone dry. He sputtered a few sounds, finally nodded.

"We want to know everything about Shabaka—"

The double shock of betrayal by his Communist masters and the police knowledge of it made Silva sag in the chair. He hid his face in his hands.

In less than a minute, without striking him once, Lyons had broken the arrogant attorney.

Furious knocking at the door interrupted the interrogation before the questions started.

"What?" Lyons demanded. "I said to leave us alone! What do you want?"

"You got a call from someone named Flor. You want me to tell her to call back later?"

16

A National Guard war-surplus Huey troopship took Able Team to El Monte, a community of Chicano barrios and light industry only a few minutes by freeway from downtown Los Angeles. Approaching the warehouse, they saw the headlights and flashing red lights of the ambulances and sheriff's patrol cars below them. White-uniformed attendants exited a building with sheeted forms on gurneys.

"Dead ones," Towers shouted to Lyons.

"I don't care who's dead," Lyons answered, also shouting to be heard over the rotorthrob. "Flor's alive."

Litter swirled in the glare of the streetlights as the Huey descended into a parking lot. Lyons jumped from the side door the moment the skids touched asphalt. Sprinting to the warehouse door, he saw two sheriff's deputies put up their hands to stop him. He dodged through them into the warehouse.

"Hey, buster! Who do you think you are?"

"Stop that clown!"

"Flor! Where are you?" Lyons shouted, ignoring the deputies rushing to seize him.

"Over here!"

A deputy with a baton confronted Lyons. Lyons pushed him aside. The deputy swung back the baton to club the ex-LAPD officer.

"Quit it!" Lyons told him. "You don't know who you're dealing with."

"Officer!" Flor Trujillo called out. She approached, limping, from behind the bullet-pocked truck, her dress bloody, a Kalashnikov slung over her shoulder. "That is my associate you are threatening—"

"Then tell him to get out of here. This area's closed to civilians," the soldier said, breathing hard.

"Officer," Flor repeated. "This is my operation. You are only here to clean up. If you continue to threaten my associate, I will be forced to request your withdrawal."

As she spoke, she shifted the Kalashnikov in her hands. Casually gripping the forestock in her left hand, she flicked the AK's safety lever up and down with her right. In the quiet after the shutdown of the helicopter's engine, both Lyons and the deputy heard the sharp clacking of the Soviet safety. She ended the argument with the final question, "Do we understand each other?"

The deputy sheriff lowered his baton. "He with you?"

Lyons rushed to Flor. She had the presence of mind to reset the AK's safety before Lyons hugged her. For almost a minute he held her, not speaking, his face in her hair, drinking the scent of her sweat with every breath.

"Carl," she whispered. "It's okay. I'm okay. It couldn't have been more than an hour or two since I saw you."

"I thought you were gone." He felt the rise and fall of her breasts against his body.

"I'm sorry," she said. "I saw the truck leaving, and I jumped on. Like a fool I didn't take one of the radios. I'm not used to working with a team."

"What happened?" Lyons finally broke the embrace.

"Did you bring my luggage? I lost my shoes. And I have to throw this dress away."

"Hey, lovers," Gadgets jived as he joined them. "We're here on business. Time to get to it."

"What was the trouble with the sheriff's department?" Blancanales asked.

Lyons laughed. "Flor had to establish exactly who is in command here. Able Team one, sheriff's department zero—"

Flor interrupted Lyons's joke. "I am in command here. Now come meet the prisoner. He's only got a few minutes before he passes out from blood loss."

They passed the bullet-riddled boxes and crates. The overhead lights shadowed a hundred black pits in the concrete walls where slugs had chipped craters.

"Looks like someone did some shooting here," Gadgets commented.

"At me," Flor said. "They thought they'd killed me. But they hadn't. When they saw me under the truck, I came out shooting. Then I tried to hide. Like a scared little girl. They did much shooting, they shot the boxes, they shot the walls, they shot the floor but not me. When they thought I was dead, one of them found me. What a surprise he got. There were only two of them left, and I got them, too. And I captured Shabaka, their leader. But he's still alive. The others, no."

Medics and deputies crowded around the prisoner. Flat on a stretcher, the middle-aged black man writhed and groaned. As one medic knotted a tourniquet above the prisoner's bullet-shattered right knee, another medic prepared an injection. Flor motioned them all away.

"No injections. No medications. I am not done with this man."

"Miss, he's in terrible pain. He could slip into shock—"

"Of course he is in pain," Flor told the concerned medic. "He has been shot."

Lyons glanced down at the wound. "Perfect. Straight through the kneecap."

"He wouldn't answer my questions," the young woman explained, "so I shot him."

Lyons looked to Gadgets and Blancanales. "What did he say then?" He laughed.

"He told me he was only a lawyer for unfortunate teenagers. So I stood on his knee. Then he did answer my questions. You—" She shouted down into Abdul Shabaka's face. "You. Murderer of children! Tell us again what is in the truck."

"Allah be merciful, I don't know what you mean. . . ."

"That's not what you said—"

"I told you nothing."

Flor stepped on the shattered knee. Shabaka flopped and twisted on the stretcher. Behind them, they heard one of the medics gasp and mutter, "Oh, good God . . . she's torturing him, somebody stop her."

One of the deputies turned to the medic. "You hear about all those college girls hacked apart? You hear about that family on the freeway?"

Shabaka gasped out the words. "The drug. Two hundred kilos. In the truck. Crossing the border. Stop the pain and I will tell you everything. . . . Stop it, stop it, stop the pain, stop—"

Leaning her weight onto the knee, Flor asked, "The truck will go to that address. Are there any codes or passwords?"

"No. The radio is coded. No one else could send a message to the truck but. . . ."

Holding the AK by the pistol grip, Flor put the muzzle to the tip of Shabaka's nose. His eyes wide with panic, he pleaded, "No, no. I am your prisoner. No!"

"Are you telling the truth?"

"Yes, I am telling the truth. Please don't shoot, I am your prisoner, I have told you everything. . . ."

Turning to the medics, Flor motioned them to resume their care. She limped away from Shabaka without a backward glance. "Now we go to the border."

"Not you," Lyons told her.

"Why not?" his lover demanded.

"Your leg. You've been shot."

"It is nothing. A bullet fragment. I took it out with my fingernails. Come, you three—" Flor signaled the three men of Able Team. "With your help, I can stop this horrible drug. We can stop all the killing and the nightmares. Come."

Barefoot, she broke into a limping run to the helicopter.

17

A sea of wind-shimmering lights defined the city of Tijuana. Straight lines of lights marked the boulevards, snaking tongues of lights marked the *colonias* of cardboard shacks in the hills and canyons. To the west, the lights of ships sparked from the vast mirror of the moonlit Pacific.

To the north, the city's lights ended abruptly at a boulevard. Then came a land of darkness and searing points of xenon white, the no-man's-land marking the southern border of the United States.

There, in the sand of the dry rivers and dust and mesquite of the hard-dirt hills, the United States border patrol fought the never-ending police action to stop the flow of Central Americans to the restaurants and factories and barrios of North America.

Every night, with the aid of all the technology of the United States—trucks, radios, remote audio sensors, infrared scanners, magnetic sensors—the officers of the border patrol arrested and deported thousands of the would-be workers.

And every night, the hopeful workers tried

again. With the skills learned through generations of poverty and revolution and repression, of running, hiding, stoic endurance of pain and hunger and disappointment and courage, the tide of seasonal immigrants surged into the no-man's-land again.

Though the violent *cholos*—street punks from Tijuana—and the *coyotes*, who smuggled the illegals for pay, forced the border patrol to carry weapons and replace their trucks' window glass with steel mesh, the officers did not consider the losing battle against the illegals dangerous. Their work became dehumanizing—every night they had to arrest, process and deport thousands of people guilty only of hope. Often they laughed at the futility of their responsibility even while they struggled to enforce the law.

"Like trying to hold back the ocean with your hands," Patrol Agent Miles said through the helicopter's intercom. "That truck you want will come through the freeway gates over there."

The hard-muscled, good-humored young agent pointed to the complex of offices and inspections booths below them where the freeways of U.S. Highway 805 and Mexico Highway 1 met at the border. The headlights and taillights of semitractor trailers carrying cargoes north and south streaked the freeways. Then he pointed to the lights of San Ysidro.

"And there's where it'll go. If you knew what the truck looked like, we could spot it at the border and follow it north. Eliminate any chance of a screw-up.''

"We don't know what it looks like," Gadgets told him. The Stony Man electronics wizard pointed to the captured long-distance transceiver. "We only have the radio. I could transmit and backscan to their signal when they answered, but they know the voice of their man. We could blow it."

"Let's wait until they show up at the drop," Lyons advised.

"When exactly do you expect the delivery of the dope?" the patrol agent asked.

Flor spoke. "They didn't say a time. The one in the truck said they were making good time north. Said they were a hundred miles south of the border."

"A hundred miles?" Miles said. "When was this?"

"Two hours ago."

"Hey, friends," Agent Miles laughed. "Your people might be waiting for you. Trucks move fast on those Mexican highways."

"The Drug Enforcement Agency's already watching the address," Flor countered. "I gave them the address when I requested the unmarked cars."

"Those unmarked cars," Gadgets asked, "will they look like cars? Or will they look like unmarked police cars?"

"No way, hombre," Miles bantered. "They'll look like people cars. Your associate—" Miles nodded to Flor "—has the right credentials. The DEA operates its own used-car lot. They use them once, then sell them off. They buy cars, sell cars, take trade-ins, and they go straight into the war on Dope International. Always good cars. We use them to put the snap on *coyotes*."

The pilot of the National Guard helicopter returned to the border patrol's base. Flor and Patrol Agent Miles went into the office to confirm, via border-patrol radio, the waiting unmarked cars and the surveillance of the drop address.

Able Team gave their equipment a final check as the helicopter's rotors revved. When Flor returned from the office, she slipped her Kevlar Windbreaker over a denim jump suit. She put the fourth secure-frequency hand-radio in one of the Windbreaker's pockets. As she strapped on a bandolier of Uzi mags, Lyons shouted to her over the rotorthrob, "We need someone to stay here to coordinate."

"If you think you must, then you must," Flor told him. "The three of us can take them without you."

"I mean you," Lyons told her.

"No!"

"You're already wounded. No more talk. Pilot, up! Take it up!"

Lyons shoved her backward out the side door. Falling to the pavement only two feet below, she grabbed at the skid as the helicopter floated away.

Lyons looked down as Flor cursed him, her words unheard over the roar of the rotorblast.

A HUNDRED FEET ABOVE the parking lot of the Drug Enforcement Agency offices in San Diego, they saw a man in a suit run through the streetlights.

He stood in the rotorstorm as the helicopter touched down. Lyons jumped to the asphalt and helped Gadgets and Blancanales unload suitcases of weapons and electronic gear. Reaching the helicopter, the DEA officer stopped them.

"I just got a report from the stake-out cars," he shouted to Able Team as the rotors turned above them. "The truck waited there for an hour or so. Then two carloads of Federals showed up and escorted the truck away."

"What!" Lyons gasped.

"Yeah, Federals they said. Described them as—" the DEA field officer read from the report "—unmarked Dodge with blackwall tires, institutional white, no trim. Antennas for radio telephones and police-band communications. Four Caucasian males. Crew cuts, suits, no sideburns, mustaches or beards. Second car was a pickup truck with blackwalls, no trim, antennas for radio telephone and police bands. Two clean-cut Caucasians in suits. What does that sound like to you?"

"Federals," Lyons agreed. "Or someone trying hard to look official. What do they mean, 'escorted'? Did they arrest them or what?"

"No, nothing like that. They helped the Mexicans back out the truck, and now they're all out on Otay Mesa Road. Our cars are keeping them in sight."

"Where does the road go?"

"The airfield."

"Got to stop them!" Lyons said as he climbed into the helicopter. They heard him shouting to the pilots.

Blancanales, swinging their equipment back into the Huey, asked two questions of the field agent. "Those Federals. They show anybody any identification?"

The agent shook his head.

"And did the agency, I mean, the Central Intelligence Agency give you any calls this morning?"

"Are you kidding? The CIA would never call us. We're only law enforcement. They're above all laws."

With a quick salute, Blancanales thanked the agent. Lyons leaned out the side door as the rotors revved to lift off. "Tell your people we're on our way!"

"What?"

Stepping onto the skid, Lyons shouted directly into the agent's ear. "Tell your follow cars we're on our way!"

Then the asphalt fell away. Standing on the skid, Lyons looked down at the rooftops and lights of downtown San Diego. Blancanales buckled on his safety harness and extended a hand to his partner.

Inside, Lyons jerked the side door closed. He shouted to his partners over the noise of the rotors and fuselage vibration, "Odds are, those Harvard boys are escorting the truck to a plane."

"Use the intercom," Gadgets shouted back.

Lyons pointed forward to the pilots. Gadgets and Blancanales nodded. They leaned close to Lyons.

"This could not be a Langley game," Gadgets told his partners. "The 'crazy dust'. The gangs. The M-16 from Vietnam. That theater for hate movies. Please tell me I'm crazy even to think this is a CIA game. Please."

"Maybe they could be Russians," Blancanales suggested.

"With the Cuban Commies cooperating to break it up?" Gadgets countered. "That doesn't help me at all. I want to believe those freaked-out right-wingers in Washington wouldn't want to start a war between black people and white people."

"Maybe it's a propaganda operation that got out of control," Blancanales said. "To make the Cubans and the Libyans and Russians look like psycho terrorists."

"Forget that talk!" Lyons told them. "There's two hundred kilos of 'crazy dust' in that truck. Towers said just one sniff of the stuff turns those punks into psycho killers. Two hundred kilos would make an army of psycho killers. An army from hell, ripping our country apart. We're stopping the truck before they load the drug on a plane. If we wipe out a CIA operation, that's their problem.''

His partners nodded. Resolved, they suited up for the fight. They put on their blood-crusted battle armor and loaded their weapons. For the three men of Able Team, the questions of responsibility for the terror and the weapons and the drug became meaningless. Whether the conspiracy originated in the Kremlin or Tripoli or within a secret clique of extremists within the United States government, their mission remained the same: protect the people of the United States.

18

Three sets of taillights streaked along the desert road. In the distance, across an expanse of empty desert, a cluster of lights and parallel lines of lights marked the location of the airfield. To the east, the horizon paled with the early false dawn of summer.

Lyons sat at the helicopter's left side door. He had taken the twenty-inch barrel from the bullet-smashed Atchisson and replaced the short barrel of his own Atchisson. With his weapon loaded with a magazine of one-ounce armor-piercing slugs, he waited.

Blancanales sat at the right side door with his M-16/M-203 over-and-under assault rifle-grenade launcher. He had loaded the grenade launcher with a high-explosive 40mm shell. A bandolier of high-explosive and phosphorous grenades crossed his black Kevlar-and-steel battle armor.

Gadgets stayed in the center, where he could pass ammunition and weapons to either side and also man the scrambled radio to the truck carrying the drugs. With the radio's power on, he, too, waited.

"Hit the lights," Lyons said into the intercom.

The pilot switched on the helicopter's xenon spotlight. Sudden noon illuminated the two-lane road. Exactly as the DEA report had described, Able Team saw a white Dodge leading the truck. A pickup truck followed.

"Tell the follow cars to fall back," Lyons said next.

Breaking in on the radio frequency of the cars that trailed the drug convoy, the pilot advised the officers of the interception. Lyons looked back. Far behind, he saw a set of headlights pull to the side of the road.

"Wizard. . . tell the scum what's happening."

Gadgets flipped up the transmit switch. "You in the truck. Stop. We are prepared to destroy if you continue. Stop or die."

He flicked off the transmit. As he waited for an answer, he called out to his partners, "Is that straight talk? Did I tell them?"

An electronically resynthesized voice answered. "Whoever you are, you are interfering in the operations of the United States government. You are hereby directed to desist from your pursuit and communication, under penalty of law."

"You got identification?" Gadgets asked.

"If we must present identification, we will arrest you."

"How do I know I'm not talking to a wetback with a Harvard accent?"

Lyons and Blancanales laughed at Gadgets's

jive. Then slugs hammered the underside of the Huey. The pilot wrenched the controls to the side.

The sudden banking threw Lyons against his safety harness. Hanging against the straps, he saw the lights of Tijuana and San Diego fall away. The turquoise of the eastern horizon appeared as the pilot righted the troopship. Gadgets's voice came on the intercom. "There's the answer. War."

Lyons spoke into the intercom. "Pilot, take us in on their right side. Quick flyby."

"What do you intend to do, sir?"

"Stop them."

"They fired at us. I don't know if I'm authorized to risk any further damage to National Guard equipment—"

"Pilot," Lyons interrupted with a question. "Were you trained for combat?"

"Yes, sir."

"Well, here it is. Take us in."

"You've got the authorization?"

"Most definitely," Blancanales answered. "You got the message from Washington, correct?"

"Stop the talk!" Lyons shouted. "Take us in!"

"But, sir, you want me to attack civilian vehicles?"

"Flyboy, if you don't want to do it, get out—"

Banking again, the Huey swept down on the

road. At a hundred ten miles an hour, the chopper gained on the speeding vehicles. Muzzle-flash sparked from the back window of the pickup.

As Lyons sighted on the pickup, the helicopter leaped in altitude, climbing to two hundred feet. Lyons yelled into his intercom, "What is your problem?"

"I'm sorry, sir. But my superiors will prosecute me."

Lyons turned to Gadgets. "Put a pistol to the back of his head." As Gadgets went forward with his Beretta 93-R in his hand, Lyons spoke again to the pilot.

"You are now at pistol point, pilot. Your superiors can't hold you responsible for your actions."

A laugh answered. "Yes, sir. I'm no longer responsible. You should have taken me hostage sooner. Here we go."

The helicopter dropped. It skimmed the desert brush. Lyons sighted on the pickup. A shadow inside pointed a rifle out the side window.

Lyons put a slug through the passenger door. The truck veered across the road, then swerved straight. Lyons hit the cab again. The driver stomped on the brakes, the pickup skidding sideways. Lyons pivoted in his seat to fire once more, but the helicopter left the truck far behind.

Autofire flashed from the white Dodge sedan. Slugs slammed the aluminum of the Huey. Lyons saw rifles firing from the passenger window. He sighted on the car and fired one slug, then another. The rifle fire stopped. He spoke into the intercom. "Pilot, other side of the road. Politician, high explosive into the truck's cab."

"Cargo truck or pickup?" asked Blancanales as the helicopter gained altitude.

"Pickup."

A streak of fire flashed past the helicopter. The pilot threw the Huey into a violent turn. Leaning against his safety harness, Lyons looked back.

The pickup truck accelerated to close the distance with the cargo truck. In the graying light, he saw a form in the back of the pickup.

Lyons spoke to Blancanales through the intercom. "A man in back's got a rocket launcher. Hit him, Pol. Pilot, take us in."

"Against rockets?" the pilot protested.

"Think of this as advanced combat training. No grades, no scores. Just pass or fail."

The pilot took the helicopter in again, this time on the left-hand side of the road. As an evasive maneuver, he bounced the troopship, rising and falling in altitude from two hundred feet to fifty feet. Blancanales struggled to aim his grenade launcher at the pickup.

The two-velocity 40mm grenade went far beyond the vehicle and exploded in the desert.

As Blancanales reloaded, Lyons screamed into the intercom, "Quit the yo-yo routine!"

"But—"

"But nothing. Take it in and hold it so my partner can make his shot."

"There's another helicopter!"

"What?" Lyons leaned far out from the side door to look back. A helicopter approached, flying at head height across the desert. It cut over the road, then banked. Lyons leaned across the Huey to look through the opposite side door.

The border patrol helicopter closed on the convoy of trucks and passenger car. Lyons shouted into the intercom, "Who's in that helicopter? Tell them the shits have a rocket launcher!"

"It's your partner, that knock-out looker—"

"Patch me through to her—"

The intercom line buzzed with static, then Lyons heard Flor's voice cursing him. "You macho son of a bitch, who the fuck you think you are to push me out of my operation? Channel is closed!"

The frequency went dead. Lyons shouted again, "Tell them about the rocket—"

As the helicopter neared the pickup truck, an autorifle flashing from the side door, the rocket launcher shot flame.

The launchflash lighted the helicopter. In a frozen instant, in the milliseconds before the RPG hit its target, Lyons saw Flor leaning from the helicopter, a rifle in her hands. Then, at an altitude of ten feet above the sand, the helicopter exploded. It hit the sand and disintegrated in a maelstrom of flame and twisting metal.

"Oh, Flor..." Lyons gasped. He unsnapped his safety harness and scrambled across the Huey, the Atchisson in his hand clattering on the aluminum floor.

In the opposite door, Blancanales beside him, he looked back to see a column of sooty flame rising from the desert. As their speed took them away from the crash, Lyons leaned farther from the side, hoping the impossible, hoping to see Flor run from the mass of fire and junk metal.

No one left the wreckage.

Blancanales grabbed one of Lyons's bandoliers and pulled him back into the helicopter. He shouted into his friend's face, "They're dead, Ironman. She's dead. And if you don't get with it, we'll be dead, and that insane drug will hit the streets. Back to your position."

Stunned, his mind reeling with the loss, Lyons obeyed. He returned to his safety harness and snapped himself in. Blancanales watched him for a moment. Lyons made no effort to put on his intercom headphones and mike. Blancanales shouted to him, taking over the leadership. "Ironman! Put on your headset! Pilot, get ready to go in again."

"But—"

"But nothing. Do as you're told or you'll be shot. Take it in so I can hit that rocket launcher. Wizard, if our pilot hesitates again, put a bullet in his head and then we'll give the copilot a try."

"Hey, weekend warrior," Gadgets jived, but

not joking, his voice hard and angry. "You heard it. You're going to die either way."

Confronted by the threats, the pilot took the helicopter down to the road. Now the two-lane road cut ruler-straight across the desert. Only a mile away, they saw the lights of the airfield. Sighting over the grenade launcher, Blancanales directed the pilot, "Down, down, hold it—" As he squeezed the M-16/M-203's second trigger, Blancanales shouted into the intercom. "Now take it up, *now!*"

As the 40mm grenade arced to the truck, the suited Anglo in the back of the pickup fired the RPG. The rocket streaked under the helicopter. Then the rocket man died in a flash of high explosive.

Out of control, the pickup left the road. Overturning in a spray of dust, the truck rolled. Blancanales looked back to see flame billow. He glanced at Lyons.

Slumping against the safety webbing, Lyons leaned his face in his hands. Blancanales reloaded his grenade launcher. He took the 40mm casing and bounced it off Lyons.

"Get with it, Ironman. Cry for her later. You're still on duty."

Without looking up, Lyons shook his head. Blancanales unsnapped his safety belt and went over to his friend. He grabbed a strut for a handhold and kicked Lyons.

Lyons did not notice. Blancanales kicked him

again and again as he shouted down into his friend's ear.

"She's dead, and there's nothing you can do to make her live again! You're alive, and you're on mission and it isn't done yet! A lot of people are going to die if we don't stop that truck. Now—"

A hand like steel clamped on Blancanales's ankle. Lyons looked up to his partner and nodded. He said nothing. He pointed down and nodded. Blancanales squatted for an instant and embraced his friend. Neither man spoke. Then Blancanales crouch-walked across the Huey and strapped himself into his seat.

"Take it down again," Blancanales told the pilot.

Below them, the white Dodge and the cargo truck raced to the airfield. Dropping to zero altitude, the pilot paralleled the truck. Autofire flashed from the sedan.

As Blancanales aimed his grenade launcher, a slug ricocheted through the cockpit. Plexiglas splintered. The helicopter veered away for an instant until Gadgets pushed the pilot's head with the muzzle of the Beretta. The helicopter returned to its parallel course.

"Steady..." Blancanales said into the intercom. Slugs hammered the helicopter. He fired and shouted. "Take it away!"

Hundreds of steel fragments slashed the front tires of the truck. Skidding sideways across the gravel airfield, the driver lost control. The truck tipped sideways and slid to a stop.

The Dodge cranked a sweeping turn. At the other end of the field, a Lear jet left a hangar.

"Now the Dodge," Blancanales told the pilot. Reloading, he looked over at Lyons.

As the helicopter banked through a steep turn, Lyons waited, his face expressionless, the Atchisson ready in his hands. He stared out at the dying, paling night as if he were a passenger on a bus. Blancanales shouted into the intercom, "Ironman, hit the Dodge with everything you can put out."

Without acknowledging his partner, Lyons took a magazine of 12-gauge rounds out of his bandolier. He held the magazine in his teeth and waited, grimacing like a pirate.

"Take us in, pilot," Blancanales said.

Swooping low, the helicopter closed on the Dodge. An Anglo in a suit leaned from the car's rear driver-side window and fired an Uzi up at the troopship. The 9mm slugs plinked the aluminum hull.

The Dodge skidded to a stop at the overturned cargo truck.

"Up to a hundred feet and hover. Hover!" yelled Blancanales. "Wizard, grenades out the doors. Everything!"

The helicopter seemed to lurch to a stop. Dust clouded from the field as Blancanales stood in the side door and fired his M-203 straight down at the Dodge.

The Dodge's driver stepped from the door of the car as the grenade hit the roof. Suddenly headless, he took one more step and fell.

While Lyons emptied his magazine of slugs through the roof of the Dodge, each impact like a supersonic sledgehammer strike, Gadgets pulled the cotter pins from hand grenades. He lobbed them out the doors underhand, then pulled two more out and threw those.

Blancanales sprayed the Chicanos and Anglos with thirty 5.56mm slugs. At the other side door, Lyons dropped out the spent magazine and loaded seven rounds of double-ought and number-two steel.

Lyons sighted on a man in a suit sprinting across the gravel. The blast sent steel through his brain and heart and lungs. He died before he fell. A Chicano scrambled from the back of the truck. Lyons put a single blast through his body. Another Chicano stepped over the corpse. Steel from the Atchisson and from one of Gadgets's grenades ripped him.

"That plane!" Blancanales called out.

The Lear jet veered away from the carnage. An arm reached from the cabin and pulled the cabin door closed. Accelerating, the jet bounced across the field.

The helicopter pilot turned the Huey. At a hundred miles an hour, he attempted to intercept the jet before it lifted off. But the jet's engines took it into the dawn sky and away.

"Sorry, I couldn't stop it, it was too fast..." the copter pilot apologized.

"Back to the truck and the car. Put us down," Blancanales said.

Nothing moved in the scene. Anglos and Chicanos sprawled around the overturned truck and the unmarked sedan. As the Huey touched down on the field, the rotorstorm made the suit coats of the dead Anglos flap.

"We need prisoners," Blancanales told his partners.

Jumping from the helicopter, they fanned out to approach the bodies. They glanced into the Dodge. They saw only blood. In the truck, they found dead men and four hundred forty pounds of a white powder in thick vinyl sacks.

None of the dead carried identification.

AFTER THE SEARCH, Lyons finally spoke, his voice emotionless, beyond despair. "I'm going back to find Flor."

"There's not going to be anything to find, nothing that you'll recognize," Blancanales told him. "Let the fire department do it."

Lyons shook his head. "She's mine. I'll get her ready, I'll...." His voice faded away. Without speaking again, he left his partners. He walked the mile back to the crash site.

Two hours later, when a Drug Enforcement Agency car came for Blancanales and Gadgets, they joined Lyons at the wreckage.

Lyons stood in the desert, his back to the morgue workers who combed the scorched metal. They found only bones and ashes. With plastic gloves on their hands, the morgue workers put the pieces of a proud, brave woman in plastic bags for later positive identification.

Lyons walked east into the desert.

ABLE TEAM

AN EXECUTIONER SERIES

9 Kill School

MORE GREAT ACTION COMING SOON!

Horrifying events are occurring in Central America today, and Able Team is right on top of them! Dick Stivers's writing, steeped in reality, dares to tell the truth about what's really happening in that war-racked part of the world.

The saga continues in the latest hot book from Stivers, *Kill School*, set in the Honduras. Once again Carl Lyons, Pol Blancanales and Gadgets Schwarz blow human vermin to bits in their own unique and crackling style. Rumblings of a hideous conspiracy to dominate North America's neighbors worsen by the second as the three justice warriors pursue the mystery to its core.

Watch for more Able Team. These are books that scorch the reader with the searing flames of real war—it takes guts to read this fabulous series!

MACK BOLAN
THE EXECUTIONER SERIES

I am not their judge, I am their judgment—I am their executioner.
—*Mack Bolan,*
a.k.a. Col. John Phoenix

Mack Bolan is the free world's leading force in the new Terrorist Wars, defying all terrorists and destroying them piece by piece, using his Vietnam-trained tactics and knowledge of jungle warfare. Bolan's new war is the most exciting series ever to explode into print. You won't want to miss a single word. Start your collection now!

Mack Bolan's

ABLE TEAM

AN EXECUTIONER SERIES

by Dick Stivers

In the fire-raking tradition of The Executioner, Able Team's Carl Lyons, Pol Blancanales and Gadgets Schwarz are the three hotshots who avenge terror with screaming silvered fury. They are the Death Squad reborn, and their long-awaited adventures are the best thing to happen since the Mack Bolan and the Phoenix Force series. Collect them all! They are classics of their kind! Do not miss these titles!

"This guy has a fertile mind and a great eye for detail. Dick Stivers is brilliant!"

—*Don Pendleton*

GOLD EAGLE

Able Team titles are available
wherever paperbacks are sold.

HE'S EXPLOSIVE.
HE'S UNSTOPPABLE.
HE'S MACK BOLAN!

He learned his deadly skills in Vietnam...then put them to use by destroying the Mafia in a blazing one-man war. Now **Mack Bolan** is back to battle new threats to freedom, the enemies of justice and democracy—and he's recruited some high-powered combat teams to help. **Able Team**—Bolan's famous Death Squad, now reborn to tackle urban savagery too vicious for regular law enforcement. And **Phoenix Force**—five extraordinary warriors handpicked by Bolan to fight the dirtiest of anti-terrorist wars around the world.

Fight alongside these three courageous forces for freedom in all-new, pulse-pounding action-adventure novels! Travel to the jungles of South America, the scorching sands of the Sahara and the desolate mountains of Turkey. And feel the pressure and excitement building page after page, with nonstop action that keeps you enthralled until the explosive conclusion! Yes, Mack Bolan and his combat teams are living large...and they'll fight against all odds to protect our way of life!

Now you can have all the new Executioner novels delivered right to your home!

You won't want to miss a single one of these exciting new action-adventures. And you don't have to! Just fill out and mail the coupon following and we'll enter your name in the Executioner home subscription plan. You'll then receive four brand-new action-packed books in the Executioner series every other month, delivered right to your home! You'll get two **Mack Bolan** novels, one **Able Team** and one **Phoenix Force.** No need to worry about sellouts at the bookstore...you'll receive the latest books by mail as soon as they come off the presses. That's four enthralling action novels every other month, featuring all three of the exciting series included in The Executioner library. Mail the card today to start your adventure.

FREE! Mack Bolan bumper sticker.

When we receive your card we'll send your four explosive Executioner novels and, absolutely FREE, a Mack Bolan "Live Large" bumper sticker! This large, colorful bumper sticker will look great on your car, your bulletin board, or anywhere else you want people to know that you like to "Live Large." And you are under no obligation to buy anything—because your first four books come on a 10-day free trial! If you're not thrilled with these four exciting books, just return them to us and you'll owe nothing. The bumper sticker is yours to keep, FREE!

Don't miss a single one of these thrilling novels...mail the card now, while you're thinking about it. And get the Mack Bolan bumper sticker FREE!

BOLAN FIGHTS AGAINST ALL ODDS TO DEFEND FREEDOM

Mail this coupon today!